THE GOA GAMBIT

ANURAG TRIPATHI

olive turtle

NIYOGI BOOKS

Published by
NIYOGI BOOKS
Block D, Building No. 77,
Okhla Industrial Area, Phase-I,
New Delhi-110 020, INDIA
Tel: 011-26818960, +91 7428978881
Email: niyogibooks@gmail.com
Website: www.niyogibooksindia.com

Editor: Shirsha Ghosh
Design: Nadeem Ahmed
Cover Design: Misha Oberoi

ISBN: 978-81-964053-9-7
Publication: 2024

Price: ₹450

Printed at Niyogi Offset Pvt. Ltd., New Delhi, India

To my father,
the original storyteller in our family.

PART 1

THE CZAR OF THE GAMBLING INDUSTRY

Flash lights lit up the casino floor as photographers went into a frenzy when the couple walked in. Jayesh Shah was dressed in a black tuxedo, a Panama hat on his head, and a Cohiba cigar in his mouth. With him was Ruby, head of client relations, in a red evening gown with a plunging neckline. Every eye in the casino turned towards them.

'Do we have everyone's attention?' Jayesh asked softly.

'Oh yeah! Perhaps a bit more than necessary.'

'Well! In that case, get rid of these photographers. I can't see a thing with these constant flashes.'

Ruby made a slight gesture with her hand and the photographers disappeared. It took Jayesh a few seconds to acclimatise his eyes to the surroundings. Almost immediately, the regulars, most of them socialites of Goa, made a beeline towards him to collect their freebies—the men shaking his hands and the women pecking his cheeks. Jayesh acknowledged each one with warmth, handing them dinner vouchers, bottles of champagne and even some playing chips. Once the freebies were distributed, they melted away into the vast halls.

'Freeloaders!' said Ruby disdainfully. 'Why do you entertain them?'

'I only throw a few crumbs at them, and for that they sing our praises in their social circles.'

Jayesh strolled slowly through the casino and the Lobby Manager followed him.

'How many people tonight?' he asked.

'Three thousand plus,' came the reply.

'What? Are you sure?'

'Boss, that's the number of entry tickets sold.'

Jayesh noted the number with a smile and changed the topic. He knew only too well what this meant.

'Anyone interesting here tonight?'

'There's a new high-roller in town. Playing with ₹1,00,000 value chips.'

'Ok. You can leave now. On your way, ask Mr Anton to see me.'

He turned to Ruby. 'Why don't you accompany him and ensure that this new kid on the block is looked after? We don't want him leaving us any time soon. I will come 'round later and meet him in person.'

'Gladly,' said Ruby. 'In any case, I don't want to be here when that creep Anton makes an appearance.'

'Ha-ha! No love lost between the two of you, is there?'

'You can say that again,' said Ruby, walking away.

Jayesh strolled around the casino floor. Every other minute, a Pit Boss ran up to him and whispered his rough ledger in his ears. Jayesh knew that the exact numbers would be on his desk the next morning, but he still liked to collect information the old way. The Pit Bosses were the nerves of the casino operation. Interacting with them directly kept him clued in to what was happening on the casino floor. No numbers could provide the insight that a Pit Boss could about the pulse of the operation.

Anton walked up to Jayesh when the Pit Bosses were all gone. He was a pompous man in charge of the physical security at the Casino. Of late, he had started assuming the role of head of administration.

'All well, Anton?' Jayesh asked.

'There was a small incident. A guy was caught marking cards on the blackjack table. Nothing we can't handle.'

'Hmm! Who caught him?'

'Nisha identified him and relayed the information to us. We did the rest.'

'Was it Nisha or Jack?'

'How does that matter, boss? In an ideal scenario, they should both be a part of the security team reporting to me. But you insist on keeping the online surveillance outside my control.'

'There is a good reason for that and you know it. So why keep bringing it up all the time? In any case, I called you because the Lobby Manager said that there are over 3000 people here tonight. I don't seem to see them, unless they are all eating buffet on the floor below.'

Anton smiled. 'You have sharp eyes, boss. We have cut additional tickets tonight in all three casinos.'

'How many in total? Is Bobby aware of this?'

'Of course he is. It was his order. We must have cut around 10,000 receipts.'

Ten thousand! The number made Jayesh grin. He had found what he wanted. 'That will be all, Anton. I better meet the high-rollers before I go back to my office.'

Fifteen minutes later, Jayesh was on a motor boat on the Mandovi River on his way towards the ship, MV Sultan. Sultan—the latest of his many acquisitions—was being retrofitted to host the largest casino in the state of Goa. Existing licensing requirements did not allow live gaming on the Indian hinterland. Consequently, all live gaming activities were carried out in the bay area on ships which had been converted into casinos.

The Sultan defined opulence of a calibre never seen before on the Indian subcontinent. Jayesh's own chamber, however, carried an understated elegance that reflected his character. He pulled off his jacket and chucked his hat as he entered, poured himself a stiff whiskey, lit a cigar and plonked onto a comfortable chair.

The latest issue of a business magazine lay on the mahogany table in front of him. He picked it up as he took a sip of the whiskey. *The Czar of the Gambling Industry*, it said in bold letters under his picture. Jayesh laughed aloud, for he knew that nothing could be further from the truth.

MAKE AN EXAMPLE OF THE WEAK

A few dingy, sparsely furnished rooms were located on the lower deck of the MV Babbar, far away from the hustle and bustle of the casino above. These were accessible through a single staircase, the entrance to which was always locked. This was the underbelly of the casino, where an alternate world existed, where laws of the outside world held no value. Much like Hades in Greek Mythology, Anton was the lord of this underworld. His word was law here and he decided who left his underworld under what circumstances.

Anton and his crew were in charge of the physical security at the casinos. Disagreements were common on the casino floor and his men were often called upon to ensure decorum. They were also responsible for guarding the vaults and the cash counters. Besides, they coordinated with the electronic surveillance department to identify cheats and frauds.

They used coercion techniques to extract confessions from their suspects; and on the rare occasion that a subject did not confess, they would torture him into submission. Hidden behind a false wall was a lockup cell from a bygone era, complete with handcuffs and chains.

Anton loved physical interrogations. They gave him an adrenaline high, got his blood flowing. Tonight, the electronic surveillance department had caught a cheat, red-handed, marking cards at the blackjack table. The crime was petty, not worth more than a few thousand rupees, but Anton intended to make an example of him. When he entered the lockup cell, the cheat smiled at him, even complimenting him on the lockup.

'Straight out of a Bollywood movie, sir,' he said. 'Should I be scared?'

Anton smiled at him.

'I gave all my money to the men outside. I have nothing left. Let me go, sir, I promise I will never come here again.'

Anton did not reply. He took off his white shirt, hung it behind the door and pulled out a small pouch of cocaine from his pocket. He cut three fine lines and snorted them in quick succession. The cheat whistled in the background, begging him to share the elixir with him.

Within a few seconds, Anton's bloodstream had absorbed the drug and he was flying high. He turned around to acknowledge the poor fellow whose hands were cuffed to the ceiling. The fool was still whistling when the first punch landed on his lower jaw. Before he had time to react, a left hook cut his upper lip. A volley of punches landed on his cheek bones and he started yelling in pain.

Soon his face was completely disfigured. He had a black, swollen left eye, Botox-swollen lips and cuts everywhere else. The only thing untouched on his face was his nose. There was method to this madness. For the grand finale, Anton held his head by the scruff of his neck and swung a right jab on his nose. Bang! His nose broke and blood spattered on the floor. As the man shrieked in pain, Anton turned around and did a quick celebratory jig. Then he landed a few more punches in quick succession to his solar plexus. The air taken out of his belly, the man struggled to breathe, coughing blood on the floor.

Anton was still punching in the air, waiting for the cheat to regain composure for his next round of onslaught, when the door opened behind him and Jack walked into the dark, dingy room. He looked bewildered at first and then horrified, for he had never seen nor imagined anything like this. Anton was taken aback. He yelled, 'What the hell are you doing here?'

Before Jack could respond, two men rushed in, held him by his arms and escorted him out. Anton was furious. He hated being disturbed in the midst of his classic act, one on which he was yet to put the final touches. 'You lucky bastard,' he yelled at the bloodied man. 'Pray to God that my mood improves by the time I return.'

He washed the blood off his hands and walked into the adjacent room where Jack was waiting. Jack let loose a volley of abuses as soon as he entered.

'Don't tell me how to do my job,' Anton retorted. 'Why are you here in the first place?'

'I just came to tell you that the sum he has stolen is no more than 5000 rupees.' replied Jack. 'You have beaten that poor fellow within an inch of his life.'

'So? Why do these cheats think twice before visiting our casino? I hope you don't think it's because of your electronic surveillance. They are afraid to come here because of me. They know the price they will have to pay if they get caught. You have to keep reminding these bastards lest they forget.'

'Five thousand rupees! For a meagre 5000 rupees you have beaten him so cruelly?'

'One must make an example of the weak. He is a professional cheat. He doesn't have a wife, a girlfriend, and for all you know, he doesn't even have a mother. No one will come looking for him. Now, if you are done with your lecture, I need to get back to business.'

'What? You are going to beat him more?'

'Go back to your surveillance room, open a can of cola and leave a man's job to me. And don't you ever come here again.'

THE TURNING TIDE

Jayesh put away the magazine after a cursory glance and was pensively chewing on a cigar that filled the room with smoke. Equations at work were evolving too rapidly for his liking. He didn't want to be the last man standing when the music stopped playing. He had burned the midnight oil for the past 10 years to create this empire of casinos. His rags-to-riches story had inspired many who found him to be an example of what a common man could aspire to and achieve in the land of opportunities that was India. With three casinos already under his belt, and a fourth one ready to be opened in a fortnight, the sun seemed to be shining brightly on him.

But Jayesh knew that the reality was very different. He was no czar. He didn't own any of these casinos. Well, he did, but only on paper. He was an employee, a poster boy, a front for his patron, Pankaj Adhikari, a leading Goan politician. For the past decade, his benefactor had given him free reign to run the business as he wished. But things have changed in the past couple of years. For reasons Jayesh could not fathom, he seemed to have lost Mr Adhikari's confidence. He wondered if his patron felt threatened by his enormous success. To all the world he may be the unchallenged king of the gambling world, but in reality, he was fighting a losing battle to retain his job.

It was over two years ago when he noticed the first signs of the turning tide. It had started with a closer scrutiny of the regular running of the casino; then, Pankaj Adhikari began to ask him more and more questions than before. He had not objected. He didn't care so long as he was allowed to run his business the way he wanted. But not objecting was taken as a sign of weakness and the questions became suggestions. That was overstepping the mandate and he was quick to point out that he had built the business from scratch and was the best man for the job. Pointing out mistakes in retrospect was far easier than making business decisions on the spot. But he had not realised that Adhikari had already made certain decisions. He had continued to pat Jayesh on the back, but within a few weeks, Adhikari's protégéé, Bobby, was appointed to manage the money laundering operations at the casino. By doing so, his boss had deliberately created an alternate power centre to challenge his authority. Bobby immediately began to assert himself and ruffle the existing dynamics. He succeeded in getting Anton, once Jayesh's confidant, to switch loyalties.

Together, Bobby and Anton were formidable adversaries, not to be taken lightly. And as for Pankaj Adhikari, he was a seasoned politician, and a politician can never be trusted.

Shaking off his pensive mood, Jayesh switched on the television to catch the news. Pankaj Adhikari was on TV. The state elections were still six months away, but the rhetoric against the casino industry had already begun. Casinos were the favourite whipping boys of the politicians. The State blamed them for almost every ill: alcoholism, drug problem, prostitution, lack of law and order and anything else they could think of. Mr Adhikari was at the forefront of the agitation, rallying masses behind him with an energetic and passionate oratory which made every word sound heartfelt and true.

He switched off the television and picked up his cell phone. It was time to find out what Mr Adhikari was up to. There was no network connection as usual. The cell phone network on the ship was very poor and they had to use the landline most of the time. It was only from a few spots that one could actually connect to the network. Jayesh stood by the little balcony of his room, and found that the call went through as the phone managed to pick up a connection. 'Boss, you are all over the television channels today,' he said, 'calling your cadre to burn down the gambling dens and sink the casino ships in the Mandovi River.'

'Ha-ha! Did you like the speech?'

'It was excellent. Very passionate, boss. I only hope that the cadre doesn't take it seriously and act on it.'

'Oh, don't worry. I have been giving the same speech for over a decade. Nothing has ever gone wrong. They will forget it in a few days. This is just a bogey to keep their minds away from other more uncomfortable issues in the state. By the way, how are the preparations coming along for the inauguration? I don't want any last-minute hiccups.'

Jayesh smiled; this was the opening he was waiting for. 'Preparations are in full swing, boss. I have booked a Bollywood star to dance at the inauguration party. I have it all under control. But this watchman you have appointed to keep tabs on me will get us into trouble someday.'

'Ha-ha! Which watchman? You are the CEO and have my full confidence. I didn't want to bother you with these mundane election matters.'

Jayesh wasn't going to give in so easily. It wasn't every day that Pankaj Adhikari's new protégéé made a blunder. 'Boss, Bobby is a newcomer and doesn't understand the dynamics of the industry.'

'Why? What's happened now? Why are you two always squabbling?' Pankaj Adhikari was irritated.

'Bobby cut tickets for 10,000 people between the three casinos tonight.'

'So? What's wrong with that? I have been pushing him for more funds. We need the money. Do you know how expensive things have become?'

'Boss, that represents almost the total daily arrival of tourists in the state of Goa. We have never had more than 3000 people at the casinos on a given night.'

'Hmm! His intentions are right, Jayesh. But I get your point. Bobby's execution leaves much to be desired.'

'I don't doubt his intentions, boss. It is this casual way of doing things that worries me.'

'But we need to act. We need more money for the elections.'

'Boss, I understand that. But we have to do it carefully and cleverly. Don't you remember what happened in the "Fodder Scam"? We can't show a two-wheeler transporting a cow, can we?'

'Don't call me with problems, Jayesh,' Pankaj Adhikari retorted, 'I need the money and I need it fast. Figure out how to do it. Put your heads together if you have to and give me a solution.'

The call was disconnected. Jayesh smiled. The talk had gone far better than his expectations. He had managed to plant the idea that Bobby was still a novice and that Pankaj Adhikari needed Jayesh, whether he liked it or not.

He walked into the room, dropped the cell phone on the table, picked up the intercom and dialled the desk responsible for issuing the tickets to the casino. 'Please ensure that the tickets are in your safe custody. They are not to be given to any person without my specific approval.'

'Not even to Mr Anton, Sir?'

'Specifically Mr Anton. Is that understood?'

'Yes, sir.'

THE BEAUTY AND HER BEAST

They called her Jill. It wasn't her real name, but it didn't matter. She was once Pankaj Adhikari's girlfriend; in the days when he was still young and a little innocent, with a mind that hadn't yet been totally corrupted. He was aggressive and impulsive, with revolutionary thoughts about changing the world, fighting for the rights of the poor and the upliftment of the masses. He was also a passionate lover completely obsessed with her beauty. She basked in the attention that he showered upon her. Every Friday night, he would strip her naked and bathe her in gold paint, just like in the movie *Goldfinger*. It turned him on to see her naked golden body. Then he made passionate love to her like an animal, again and again till the early hours of the morning, or until one of them had collapsed from sheer exhaustion.

But, with the passage of time, as he started gaining power, Pankaj Adhikari changed. The young hot-headed revolutionary leader who wasn't scared to take on the world slowly turned into a seasoned politician. The aggression and impulsiveness of youth was tamped down and logic and patience were used as much as possible. There was no innocence in his words or actions anymore. Every word, every action was well reasoned, for a purpose, with an objective in mind. He had understood the futility of trying to change the world. These were good textbook ideas, which could be drummed up before elections to garner votes, but were never meant to be implemented. There were too much comfort and money riding on maintaining the status quo. In this transactional, logical world, there was no place for love. Love was an emotional response which had no logical basis. There was no justification in loving another person. Lust, on the other hand, had a logical grounding. Thus, it was only fair that love made way for lust. Lust for power. Lust for wealth. Lust for the human flesh. In his new avatar, he didn't love her anymore. He only lusted after her body, and that body was getting older with every passing year. One day, he simply told her that he was getting married to another woman. She was shocked. She had assumed that he would marry her someday.

'What about me,' she asked angrily. 'Why can't I be your wife?'

'You cannot,' he replied.

'Why not?' she yelled. 'I am good enough to be your girlfriend, but not your wife?'

'Because you don't have the right family background,' he shouted back.

It was clear that she was going to lose him to another woman. She began to wail, tears running down her cheeks, completely heartbroken.

'It's nothing,' he said, trying to placate her. 'It's an arrangement to further my political career. You are the one that I love.'

But no matter what he said, the tears continued to roll down her cheeks. She knew at that moment that her life would now move in an entirely different direction. It would never be the same again. From being his girlfriend, who was always by his side, she would now become his mistress, relegated to the shadows, never to be seen with him in public. She would no longer enjoy legitimacy. Their relationship would now be considered immoral.

On Pankaj Adhikari's wedding night, she decided to end her life. She sent him one last message before she tried to slit her wrists. But her hands trembled. She didn't have the courage to go through with the act. She wept at her helplessness. When he received the message, Pankaj Adhikari rushed to her house, dressed in his wedding sherwani, leaving his newlywed bride to fend for herself. He broke into her room and within minutes, they were hugging and kissing. Then the sherwani was half-opened-half-torn as it was removed passionately and flung across the room. Everything was as it should have been on the first wedding night—the excitement, the passion, as two human bodies impatiently explored each other. An hour later, their naked, exhausted bodies lay tangled on the bed. Everything was in order except that the woman he made love to wasn't his wife.

'The marriage is a sham,' he reiterated. 'It is you that I want.'

Jill still had a thousand questions that needed answering, but in that moment, she embraced him. She wanted to believe him. She had dedicated her life to him and had nowhere else to go. She wanted to believe him because she had no choice. It was a mistake. There was no love in his actions that night. There was only lust.

Once she accepted her status as his mistress, it was downhill all the way. He would drop in at odd hours of the day, away from the public eye, to satiate his lust. They spoke very little. He showed little commitment to their relationship. Every time she tried to engage him in a discussion, he would cut her off. He had no interest in what was happening in her life. She was merely a sex-object who satisfied his lust. Jill kept hoping that he would change with time, that the old lover would emerge again, but it only got worse. She began to complain. He called her a nag.

'Why do you keep nagging me? Don't I take care of you?'

It was true that she had his money. She had a place to live in, for which he paid. He gave her a monthly allowance which was more than enough to take care of her needs. But she didn't have him. She wanted him. She wanted to spend more time with him. She wanted to feel loved and cared for. But that was not on offer. She wondered if love had ever been a part of the equation or she had just imagined it. As their arguments increased, so did his absences. He even began to skip their Friday ritual which they had unfailingly practised for so long. It didn't matter how much gold paint she wore; it just wasn't the same as before. There was no passion in the lovemaking. The act seemed forced and laborious. She was losing him and she could sense that she was no longer the only mistress in his life. It was only a matter of time now.

One Friday evening, when he didn't turn up, she called him and insisted that he come or she would go over to the flat he had above his office. An argument erupted between them and finally, in exasperation, he said, 'Come, if you wish, but you won't be the only one. There will be two other women.'

'How dare you treat me like this?' she yelled. 'What do they have that I don't?'

'Darling,' he laughed. 'They are young and beautiful.'

The bubble finally burst. Jill had to face the reality—that he had never loved her, he had only loved her body. She threw the gold paint into the dustbin, swearing never to wear it again. Then she stripped off her clothes and stood before the mirror. She saw the reflection of a woman who was tired. For the first time, she noticed the tiny wrinkles on her face and acknowledged that her body was past its youthful glory. But now, Jill did not cry. She had dedicated her life to him. But no more. Now she would wait for the day when he was at his most vulnerable. Then, she would strike.

A GAMBLER ONCE MORE

Just a decade earlier, Jayesh's life had been very different. He had been a carefree professional gambler living out of a suitcase, travelling the world, looking for opportunities to exploit. It was roulette at Monte Carlo one day, craps in Vegas soon after, and horse racing in Hong Kong after that. It wasn't the most stable life, but it was exciting and the only life he knew; the only life he found worth living.

The carefree nomadic life had its cons. He struggled with women. Not with sex; he got plenty of that. But with companionship. He attracted women, more than he could handle, but within a matter of weeks, they would run far from him. The longest that a woman ever survived with him was five months. The poor soul was a nervous wreck by the end of it, unable to deal with his roller-coaster lifestyle. Imagine, sipping a five-thousand-dollar bottle of Romanée-Conti one night, and finding oneself practically begging on the streets the very next. But that was his life. As far as Jayesh was concerned, things were just fine, until, on a trip to Goa, he ran into Pankaj Adhikari for the first time.

He was playing roulette at one of his casinos and winning too often. This had not gone unnoticed. On the fourth night, the security team caught him just as he was about to encash his chips. They held him in custody and tried to frighten him into confessing to cheating. They had nothing against him except that he was winning far too often. Jayesh wouldn't break. He was used to taking heat from casinos all over the world and this was child's play in comparison. After two hours of pressurising him, they gave up. Jayesh was still silently gloating over his victory when a simple, unassuming looking man walked into the detention room. He was Pankaj Adhikari.

'We have been watching you, Mr Shah,' he said. 'You have an affinity for numbers.'

Jayesh smiled politely, but said not a word. It was late, he was tired. He wanted to get to his bed. But Pankaj Adhikari wasn't finished.

'I am looking for a person to run my casino business. You appear to fit the bill.'

'What?' exclaimed Jayesh, incredulous. 'Why?' he asked. He was not interested in the answer; he could not believe what he had heard and just wanted to leave.

'You are flamboyant, have a magnetic personality. You are good with numbers and understand the psychology of gamblers. These are the perfect traits for someone managing the casino floor.'

'Sir, thank you for the compliment, but I am not interested. Now, if you are done, please give me my money so that I can be on my way.'

'Of course! I was getting to that. You see, you have a choice: take my offer and you can walk out of here on your own legs, alive. Refuse my offer, and we will cut you into small pieces and feed you to the fish. Oh! And mind you, in neither of the options will you walk out with the money.'

This sudden turn in conversation amused Jayesh and he grinned. It was all so surreal. But then he looked into Pankaj Adhikari's eyes and realised it wasn't a joke at all. He was a seasoned poker player and knew that this man was not bluffing. The next moment they were shaking hands. Not because he was convinced that this was a great offer, but because he wanted to live. He hoped for a better end to his illustrious life than being fed as bait to fish. Later that night, he even contemplated running away. But the thought of living in fear for the rest of his life, always looking over his shoulder, dissuaded him.

To his utter surprise, within a few weeks he had begun to enjoy his new job. It provided him with financial stability and an opportunity to work in the casino industry. Casinos were the soul of his life. This new role required him to be well dressed, sip cocktails and shake a leg with the high and mighty of the city. It was a job that played to his strengths. Pankaj Adhikari had a keen eye for spotting talent. Over the next year, Jayesh used his considerable experience of casinos and his untapped acumen to turn the business around. From being a lowly watering hole for the drunks of the city, he transformed it into a chic place for the young and trendy. Anyone who was anybody in the city of Goa wanted to be seen there. A job which had been thrust upon him helped him realise his own potential and he found it a lot of fun. Ten years passed smoothly and successfully as his business grew many folds, making a huge amount of money for his patron. In return, Pankaj Adhikari gave him a decent amount of money, but nothing commensurate to the wealth he had created for his patron.

Money laundering was always at the core of the casino operation. When Pankaj Adhikari decided to hand over the keys to the clandestine operation to Bobby, Jayesh knew that his coffin was being prepared. At first, he was angry. He had sacrificed 10 years of his life and had transformed the seedy gambling dens into swanky glamourous places. But he soon reconciled to the situation. After all, he had little say in the matter, just as he had no say in whether he wanted to run the casinos or not. The money laundering operations were risky and had to be carried out carefully. One misstep and the entire establishment would come tumbling down, attracting the attention of every regulator in the country, from the Income Tax Department to the Enforcement Directorate.

Bobby was smart, but he was a cowboy. He was not only aggressive but also impatient, always hungering for more. He reminded Jayesh of himself many years earlier, shooting first and asking questions later. On the other hand, Jayesh was now in a very comfortable position. Ten years of hard work had earned him both money and status. His risk-taking appetite was much lower than what it used to be in the past. But he was not yet at a point where he wanted to hand over the business and retire. He did not like losing control of the money laundering operation. He knew that he was slowly and surely being forced out. On paper, he was still the owner of the casino. One wrong move by Bobby could get him into big trouble. So, he had decided that he needed to get out of the business and he had to find a way to do so on his own terms, without raising the slightest suspicion. Jayesh Shah had become a businessman for the past ten years. His gambling skills had rusted a bit, but, like cycling, once learnt they are never forgotten. All he needed now was a cache of money to start afresh.

THE PHONE KEPT RINGING

An almost empty bottle of gin, along with a few cans of tonic and soda, lay on the table in front of the sofa on which Bobby and Anton were sitting. The ashtray overflowed with cigarette butts. Although it was early in the evening, they had been drinking for some time.

'With every passing day, my respect for your boss declines,' said Bobby. 'I had high expectations, having heard so much about him.'

'He is getting old and has lost his fire. His belly is full, there is no hunger left,' replied Anton.

'Son of a bitch was bad mouthing me behind my back. If you are a man, stand up and say what you want to my face.'

'Oh, he will not confront you. It is not his style. But he is a poker player.'

'Why doesn't he abandon the throne? He is fading anyway.'

There was silence for a while. Anton downed his gin and tonic and took a long drag of the cigarette. He looked at Bobby and said, 'Thrones are never abandoned. You have to take them by force.'

Another silence followed as Bobby mulled over the statement. This wasn't a discussion he wanted to engage in. Changing the topic, he said, 'You have been with him from the beginning, haven't you?'

'I was his right-hand man. He did the thinking and I did the execution.' Anton paused to look at his cellphone which had started ringing. He glanced at the number and disconnected, then looked up at Bobby, and continued, 'We set up this business together.'

'Tell me, Anton, was he always like this?'

'No. He wasn't. There was a time when his mere presence on the casino floor sent everyone's pulse racing. He was ruthless, people feared and respected him.'

'What happened?'

The phone rang again, Anton again glanced at the number and disconnected.

'Go ahead, take the call,' said Bobby. 'It might be urgent.'

'Boss, no one owes me money,' replied Anton. 'If someone is trying to reach me urgently, he will call again. What is it that you were saying?'

'I was asking you what happened. Why did Jayesh change?'

'The environment has changed over the past decade. From being gambling dens, casinos have evolved into an entertainment industry. Dark interrogation rooms have given way to electronic surveillance, bank credit has replaced mob money.'

'So you think Jayesh changed to fit into the new industry environment?'

'Yup. But I still believe in the ways of the old world. Casinos are not and should not be seen as means of entertainment. They represent a serious business.'

'Is that the reason you two have drifted apart?'

'That's only one of the reasons. I have been sidelined from being his right-hand man. I no longer enjoy his trust.'

'Who sidelined you? Jack?'

'Yeah! Amongst others. These days, boss prefers the company of brains over muscle. You know, the guys who talk smart. All Jack does is sit inside an air-conditioned room drinking cola while I do the running around.'

'Doesn't Jack report to you?'

Bobby had touched a raw nerve and Anton exploded. 'No! He doesn't. I tell you, that son of a bitch should be reporting to me.'

'I am surprised he doesn't report to you.'

'I have asked boss on many occasions, but he denies my request every single time.'

'What about Ruby? She seems close to him. She doesn't seem too brainy. What's her story?'

'She is a climber. I knew it the first time I saw her.'

'She is very attractive.'

'Hahaha! Attractive, my ass. If only you knew the truth.'

'What truth?'

'Let's just say, she isn't your type.'

'What do you mean, Anton? Be clear. You are irritating me.'

'Only two people know this,' Anton said. 'You are the third. She stands up and pisses.'

'Excuse me?' said Bobby, looking shocked.

'Yeah! You heard me right,' said Anton, laughing hysterically. 'She is a ladyboy.'

'What the fuck is she doing in Goa?'

Before Anton could reply, his phone rang again. This time he disconnected without even looking at the screen and went on, 'Boss fell for her beauty, much like yourself, before he discovered who she really was. When I came to know, I wanted to put her back on the return flight the same day she had arrived. But he stood by her and she managed to hold on.'

'Hmm! A ladyboy heading our escort service? She is a survivor. And all that attitude! I am going to enjoy dealing with this one,' said Bobby, with a smirk.

'Boss, she threw attitude at me once. I put a knife to her throat that very night and threatened to cut her into pieces and feed her to the fishes in the Mandovi. You have to keep these types on a tight leash.'

'You sure have your own way of dealing with people, Anton. I am glad we are on the same side.'

'Thank you, boss.'

'I hear you still have an interrogation room on the lower deck of MV Babbar?'

'Come on, boss,' said Anton with a wide grin. 'It's all show now. Not like the old times.'

'If you say so,' replied Bobby.

'But I tell you, boss, we need to bring back the old ways. It is good for business. Give them whatever they want—money, women, drugs and alcohol. Entice the bastards and then let them loose on the casino floor. No rules, no limits, no holds barred. But if they default, then no sweet talk. Do as I say and we can double our revenues. One month is all I need to clean up this place.'

'I hear you, Anton, loud and clear. But first, we must wait for an opening to strike.'

'Wait is all we do here these days,' said Anton, getting up impatiently from his chair and punching in the air. 'There is no action.'

'Don't lose patience,' replied Bobby. 'An old lion is still a lion. A hyena that takes him casually will pay for it with its life.'

'I am a man of action. I don't understand these worldly matters. What do you suggest we do?'

'We must strengthen our position. For that, I need the cash flows to improve. Since the tickets are no longer in our possession, how do you propose we do it?'

'We can increase the number of tables on which offset bets are being played.'

'But I thought that Jayesh didn't allow more than two operational tables per casino?'

'Yeah, he doesn't. But I am the one who manages the floor.'

'Are you sure it can be done? That will be really helpful.'

'Consider it done, boss.'

Anton stood up to leave and glanced at the message on his mobile phone as he walked out. It read, 'Bastard, don't you value your life?' He closed the door of his chamber and went straight to the bathroom, pulled open the vanity mirror above the wash basin, and reached for the first-aid box that lay in the cavity there. A gram of cocaine packed neatly in a small pouch lay inside the box. He ripped the packet and dumped the contents on the glass-topped coffee table. Using his credit card, he spread the contents evenly and cut them into 3 fine lines. Then, he pulled out a crisp 500 rupee note from his wallet and rolled it. Putting one end of the rolled banknote into his nostrils, he snorted up the fine lines of cocaine one by one. Once the last milligram of cocaine was inside his bloodstream, he passed out.

All this while, his phone continued ringing in the background.

FROM PREY TO PREDATOR

Anton was not always built strong. He was born frail and weak, the only child in a poor family. His father was a waster, addicted to smack and alcohol. It was his mother who showered him with love and shielded him from the toxicity of life, making an otherwise unbearable life liveable. She would pick up odd jobs in the neighbourhood trying to make ends meet. But, no matter how hard she worked, money was always in short supply. It didn't help that she had a husband who—without any concern for their welfare—kept asking for money to satisfy his addiction. Every time his thirst for smack became unbearable, he would beat her in anger. It was the same when he was drunk. Anton was only five years old when he intervened for the first time, no longer able to watch the beatings go unabated. He was so badly beaten that he remained incapacitated for the next three days. However, as soon as he recovered, he intervened again. Beatings became a part of his life thereafter.

When he was 9 years old, he was woken up in the middle of the night by sounds of loud wailing. As expected, his father and mother were fighting again. However, this time it was different. He had never seen his mother so furious. She was fighting tooth and nail, kicking and scratching her husband who was much larger in size than her. Apparently, a week earlier, his father had found a small treasure trove hidden behind one of the cupboards in the house. He had quietly taken the money and spent it on his addiction. This fact had just come to light. Anton's mother had been diligently saving the money to pay for his school fees.

Anton stood up and lunged at his father's back, trying to reign him. But he was no match for his father's strength. He was thrown a few feet away and he passed out as his head hit against the wall. He didn't know for how long he remained in that state, but after he regained consciousness, he saw his father strangulating his mother, who was kicking her legs in the air, fighting for every last breath of air. Anton has a memory lapse of what happened next. He only remembers sitting on top of his father's chest, covered in blood with a knife in his hand, shivering and crying hysterically. He had saved his mother and that is all that mattered. By the time the cops arrived at the crime scene the next morning, Anton's mother had not only removed all evidence of her son's involvement in the crime but also confessed to murdering her husband. There was sympathy for the case as everyone knew that her husband was an alcoholic wife-beater. The case was fought pro-bono by a defence lawyer. Anton's mother got a reduced sentence of four years in a local prison. Social service took custody of Anton and sent him to a shelter home.

They say that most hardened criminals can trace their beginnings to a shelter home. Anton's own experience lived up to that reputation. He was immediately preyed upon by the older boys. Every time he retaliated, they beat him up mercilessly. He realised quickly that strength was in numbers and the only way to survive was to join a gang of boys. However, none of the existing gangs would have him. Why should they? He had nothing to offer. He was neither rich nor physically strong. Thus, he had no choice but to spend the first few months hiding in the shadows. He would quickly eat his daily ration before someone took it forcibly. Then he would either go into hiding or remain in full view of the authorities. He utilised every bit of free time to work on his frail body, lifting weights, exercising. He seldom slept at nights as that was the time when he was the most vulnerable. He made sure that he was never caught alone in the toilet. By following the above regimen, Anton gave himself time to work on his body. As he developed muscles, attacks on him declined. Soon, a gang of boys accepted him and he went on to prey upon the other weaklings at the shelter home.

It was all good going for the next three years until one day he heard the sad news of his mother's passing. She had contracted tuberculosis and by the time the jail authorities heeded to her requests for hospitalisation, it was too late. Thus, the shelter which was supposed to be a temporary abode became a permanent home for Anton and its occupants his only family. However, as Anton became an adult, he was thrown out of the shelter home along with a few other boys of similar age to fend for themselves on the streets of Goa. This was the time when Pankaj Adhikari, aggressively expanding his empire in Goa, was on the lookout for muscle power. He gladly took Anton and the other boys under his wings and used them to intimidate his business rivals into submission. However, unlike the other boys who were nothing more than street thugs, Anton shined in the eyes of Pankaj Adhikari as a fearless, ambitious foot soldier who could get the job done.

A few years later when Pankaj Adhikari came across Jayesh Shah and offered him to run his casinos, he asked Anton to trail the newcomer. However, Anton was good at identifying rising power centres and quickly aligned himself with Jayesh to become an indispensable part of his organisation, rising swiftly through the ranks to become the head of the physical security division.

THE JOURNEY FROM ARTHIT TO RUBY

Ruby was not her real name. She was named Arthit when she was born, a male child raised by a single mother in a small village on the outskirts of Chiang Mai in North Thailand. She had never known her father. Some said that the lack of paternal influence along with overwhelming maternal love had made her effeminate from an early age. But Arthit had always known who she was: a woman trapped in a man's body. Her mind and heart had never been at peace with her male form. She was only four years old when she began to express herself. By the age of seven, she had grown her hair and was stealing makeup from her mother's vanity box. It was clear to her mother where her heart lay. Arthit showed early signs of becoming a *kathoey*, an effeminate gay male, or in popular parlance, a 'ladyboy'.

By the age of twelve, she had grown into a fine, young, beautiful girl, devoid of breasts, with a tall, petite frame, and a pretty face. She was not only accustomed to compliments about her beauty from the womenfolk in the village, but also drew the attention of men. With the onset of puberty, she began to see boys in a different light. It excited her to see them by the pond in their underwear and enjoyed hugging them whenever she could.

By the age of fifteen, she realised that she could no longer blindly follow her instincts. The gap between what she desired and what she had was expanding. She needed guidance in the ways of the *kathoey*—an elder sister, a mentor. She approached an older *kathoey* from school and requested her to become her elder sister. Thus began a relationship of trust and reverence that guided her through the most formative years of her life. Amongst the first things she learnt to do was to take oestrogen-based hormones, which, amongst other changes, facilitated the development of breasts. This was followed by a change in the way she dressed, her hairstyle, shoes and makeup. Then came the question of her name.

'What would you like to call yourself?'

'Ruby.'

'Why Ruby? That isn't a Thai name.'

Ever since childhood, Arthit had admired the ruby ring worn by her mother. It was the only valuable item in her possession. 'It is the only object of beauty that I have ever known.'

And thus, Ruby was born.

After completing school, Ruby left for Chiang Mai to explore employment opportunities. She found to her dismay that people in the big city were less accepting of *kathoeys*. Jobs were difficult to come by and the ones that did come her way were all temporary. After spending a little over two years doing temporary jobs that did little good for her ego or wallet, Ruby decided to travel to Bangkok in search of greener pastures. Her mother did not approve. She knew only too well what happened to young girls coerced to migrate to the megacity. But Ruby was able to convince her, arguing that she wasn't migrating under coercion, that she was educated enough to make informed decisions, that as soon as she found a good job, she would start sending money home. But luck seldom obliges the poor and needy. After walking all over the city in search of work for over a month, all she could find was the job of a waitress at a café. The money was barely enough for her to survive, let alone save and send back home. But the job provided her with a footing in the city till something better came along.

Then a chance conversation with another waitress sent her exploring to Patpong, a tourist hotbed in Bangkok. Whilst most of the establishments were Go-Go Bars selling sex, there were a select few that were merely watering holes for the thirsty traveller. The owner at one of these bars took a liking to her. He could see potential and offered her a job as a waitress with special duties. 'All you have to do is chat with the customers and sell them drinks,' he told her.

'That's all?' She was suspicious. 'No sex?' she asked, blurting out what was playing on her mind.

'No,' he replied. 'We don't sell sex. If a customer wants to take you out, that's between you and him. He will have to pay us, of course.'

'What do I get for this?' she asked.

'A small retainer for your loyalty to this bar, and a cut on the drinks you sell.'

That sounded fair. In any case, selling drinks was more interesting than selling coffee. She resigned from the café that night and moved to Patpong, chatting up customers and selling drinks.

Drinks is all she sold for two months. But, like many well-intentioned girls from poor families, temptation, which was always lurking in the shadows, seduced her soon enough. Prostitution was a way of life in Patpong, a norm amongst the people that worked and lived there. Being surrounded by such an environment numbed a person to the stigma associated with it. She had seen many of her colleagues go on night-outs and return in the morning looking no worse off, with money in their pockets. After deliberating for days on end, she finally agreed to go on a night out with an American, a frequent customer of the bar who had taken a liking to her. While dining at an expensive restaurant that evening, she told him that she was a *kathoey*. The disappointment was clearly visible on his face. He didn't allow it to come in the way of the dinner; but the dinner was not followed by a visit to his hotel.

Ideally, she should have been happy; she had managed to earn good money without selling her body. Instead, she had mixed feelings about the evening. It was clear that the hotel visit didn't happen because she was a *kathoey*. So when a few days later the American invited her again for an expensive dinner, followed by a visit to a fancy hotel, she was thrilled. She returned home the next morning with 3000 Baht in her pocket and a set of new clothes, the burden of morality no longer pressing on her shoulders. Such was the fate of many poor women who came to Bangkok in search of a living. Soon, her mother started getting regular instalments of money. She was pleased with the support that her daughter provided and didn't ask uncomfortable questions.

A year later, Ruby threw away whatever little was left of her morality and moved to a popular Go-Go Bar at Soi Cowboy. One night, while she was pole dancing to a raunchy number, her vivacious body gyrating seductively to the music, her eyes full of life and an enticing smile on her face, Jayesh spotted her. She didn't like him at first. Indian men were generally aggressive and uncouth, haggling over every penny. When you thought that the deal had been struck, they haggled on the goods on offer. 'I want you twice in that much money,' was a common ask. But, Jayesh made her an offer she couldn't refuse.

'Food, lodging and 50,000 Baht per month retainer. Whatever you earn on top is yours to keep.'

Fifty thousand Baht! Had she heard him right, or was God playing games with her like he had all her life? This could help her fulfil her deepest desire, to become a proper woman. The final frontier to becoming a woman was a surgery involving the realignment of genitalia. This was the Mount Everest for *kathoey*s, the ultimate life goal vehemently desired; and there was a clear divide in the community between the 'haves' and the 'have-nots'. With this kind of money, she could save enough to get the surgery done within two years...

She was still dreaming about her body when she heard Jayesh say, 'Is the offer acceptable to you?'

She wondered for a moment whether she should tell him the truth about herself before accepting the offer. But what if he changed his mind? Such an opportunity had never come her way before. 50,000 Baht a month was too big a sum to fuck around with. Besides, working in a casino would be a whole new experience.

'Yes', she said, her eyes shining. 'Thank you.'

ONLY ETHICS MATTERED

Karishma examined the parcel addressed to her editor that lay on her desk. The sender had not put down their name. Nothing unusual about that. Most whistle-blowers liked to remain anonymous. Some revealed themselves at a later stage when they got comfortable with the reporter; but many never revealed themselves at all. She went through the contents of the parcel, trying to gage its credibility, reading the enclosed letter twice. Then she went to see her editor, brimming with excitement.

Karishma had always wanted to be a journalist. She believed that in the right hands, a pen was truly mightier than the sword. Hence, at 20, having finished her undergrad in English Literature, she joined a news daily as one of its youngest reporters. What she lacked in experience, she more than made up for in passion and diligence. Armed with a pen and diary, and an open, inquisitive mind, she set out every morning to find new stories. On the surface, people led mundane boring lives.

But, if one dug a little deeper, there were stories waiting to be found everywhere. Her unique approach brought her accolades from colleagues and seniors alike. But then she hit a road block. She was asked to drop a story. When she wanted to know why, there was no clear reply. The editorial department had liked the story, it was the commercial department which had struck it down. Her story was too damning of a large corporate house which was an important advertiser in the newspaper.

Karishma refused to retract her story, despite knowing that her stand would get her into trouble. Her editor tried to instil some real-world sense into her, telling her not be egoistic. 'Don't take a stand,' he told her, 'this is not a battle you can win.' But this wasn't about her ego. It was about ethics. This was the reason she had become a journalist in the first place. If she didn't stand for the truth, she might as well do something else. Finally, there was no option but to resign. She served her notice period and then went to look for a new job, feeling assured that with her track record, she would easily find one. But weeks became months and she realized that it wasn't going to be easy. She interviewed at many media houses. The interviews always started on a good note, but somewhere midway they went downwards, usually at the point when she was asked why she had left her previous organisation. Once she told them the truth, their interest evaporated. Nobody said that she was wrong. How could they? She had stood her ground on ethics and truth. How could they find fault with that? They all carried such words on their mastheads. These were the right words. Except, they weren't very practical in today's world and were seldom practised anymore.

After struggling for nearly six months interviewing at one media house after another, a friend recommended that she meet the editor of *Satya* (Truth), a weekend newspaper. It was crowdfunded and hence, independent of the corporate houses that controlled much of the news in circulation. At the interview, she was once again asked the now familiar question. She replied in a sarcastic undertone that she had resigned because of her strong belief in the truth. She expected the interview to end on the same note as many others before it. It was only when the editor laughed and narrated her own story, that she realised she had finally found her dream job. That was two years ago. Since then, she has uncovered many stories, increasing the subscription of the weekend daily almost three folds. There were still people out there who wanted to read real news and learn the truth irrespective of how damning it might be. But credibility also brought added responsibility on the shoulders of the people writing the stories. They had to be certain of their facts and careful that they weren't playing into anyone's hands.

'This thing is explosive,' Karishma said to her editor, placing the parcel on her desk.

'I know, but where is the evidence?' asked her boss.

'Yup. There is no evidence to corroborate the story.'

'So why are you looking so excited?'

'I believe this story. It is consistent. This person has either lived this life, or seen it up close with her own eyes.'

'What if we are playing into the opposition's hands? The elections are only a few months away.'

'That thought did cross my mind. But I still feel it is worth pursuing.'

'Go ahead. But be discreet. No allegation unless we have evidence. Remember, we only uncover the truth.'

THE LOST INNOCENCE

Some people are born with good looks. Some are born with intelligence. Very few are born with both these qualities. Nisha was one of them. No wonder she was a great asset for the casinos. People who saw her for the first time wondered if she was a film star. With her looks and sense of style, she could easily have been one. But it were Nisha's parents who were actors. Her father was a Bollywood star and her mother a revered theatre personality. Both had achieved much recognition and fame in their professional lives. Their marriage was supposed to be a match made in heaven. With so much love and passion, what could go wrong? But sometimes, love isn't enough. Their honeymoon was short-lived. Within a few months, love had disappeared and passion had turned into anger. By the time Nisha came into the world, they fought constantly, seldom agreeing on anything. She often wondered whether her birth was unplanned, the result of a night gone horribly wrong. But it wasn't an accident; it was a deliberate act bereft of logic or thought, riding heavily on hope and miracle. They hoped that the coming of a child would bring them closer to each other, that it would help them sort out their differences, and bring light where there was only darkness. It was a half-hearted attempt bound to fail, for hope alone seldom achieves anything in life. The friction between them only increased with the coming of their beautiful daughter. The constant fighting took a toll on both her parents, but more so on her mother. Initially, Nisha's mother fought tooth and nail with her husband, defending her point of view and protecting her way of life. But, with the passage of time she began to tire and her will to fight withered.

The final battle lines were drawn between them when Nisha was only four years old. Her successful father decided that she would follow in his footsteps and become a movie star. Her mother vehemently opposed the idea. She held their celebrity status responsible for destroying their married life. She wanted to protect her daughter's innocence. She wanted Nisha to live the life of a normal child, cocooned from the burden of expectations, fame and glamour. But her protests fell on deaf ears. Her husband's ambitions were far too strong. And so, Nisha spent much of her childhood in closed rooms. While children her age were chasing butterflies in the garden and exploring the world around them, she was attending dance lessons. Acting classes followed a few years later. She grew up a lonely child, isolated from the world around her, with hardly any opportunities to make friends of her age.

Her mother watched in frustration as her child's innocence and laughter was crushed under the burden of her father's expectations. The pressure of a failed marriage together with the guilt of not being a good mother ate away at her and she sought respite in drugs, alcohol and gambling.

Nisha was intelligent and diligent. She excelled in all her classes although she had no real interest in them. She longed wistfully to play with children her age in the playground and parks after school, but on her father's insistence, she was whisked away from one class to another all the time. And as she entered her teens, she began to question her regimented life. If she had the support of her mother, perhaps she could have put up a fight. But, by then, her mother was incapacitated by drugs and alcohol and in no position to fight for her daughter.

One evening, Nisha returned from her dance class to find the lifeless body of her mother hanging from the ceiling fan. She held on to her mother's feet and wailed. Her life changed forever that night. The innocence of the child gave way to the stubbornness of a teen. A rebel was born who despised everything about her life, and most of all, her father, whom she held responsible for her mother's death. She never went back to her dance lessons.

During the last few years of her life, Nisha's mother had taken refuge at the casinos at Goa. Nisha gladly accompanied her mother on these visits. While not allowed on the casino floor, she had an outlet to meet and play with children her age who came from different backgrounds and cultures. For someone who lived a regimented life, this was a fairy-tale world. In the evenings before dinner, her mother would pour herself a large drink and sit down to play rummy with her daughter. Nisha had an eye for cards and seldom lost. While these games were friendly in nature, a point system was kept, converted into rupees at the end of the trip. Nisha always came back from Goa trips with her purse full, money that was hers, money that was not known to her father.

After her mother's passing, Nisha regularly ran away from home into the arms of her fairly-tale world. The casinos at Goa were sympathetic to her cause, having played the nanny to her for so many years. However, being a minor, her visits were short lived. It was finally on her 18th birthday that she ran away from home for good, this time with a bag full of cash from her father's locker, money that she put to good use at the casino.

GIVE HIM SOME SLACK

Jayesh was going through the invitation list prepared for the launch of the new casino. He was amused to notice that in one part of the list, every third person had a similar sounding surname, reflecting the rural background to which they belonged. Balwant had already confirmed his participation, along with his entire group of a dozen villagers. So, had Kumar Saurabh and most of the other high-rollers. He was still perusing the list when the door to his chamber opened. Looking up, he was surprised to find Jack there. He glanced at his watch. It was only mid-afternoon.

'Isn't it a bit early for you to be here? Is everything all right?' he asked.

'No, it isn't, boss. I didn't sleep very well last night.'

'Shoot. What's bothering you?'

'Did you approve an increase in the number of tables being operated by Bobby?'

'Which tables? I did no such thing.'

‘I knew it! Son of a bitch was lying.’

‘Who was? Who told you to increase them?’

‘Anton, who else? He came looking for me yesterday. He asked me to switch off the circuit cameras covering five specific tables in each of the three casinos.’

‘You mean 15 tables in total?’

‘Exactly.’

‘Is that so?’ drawled Jayesh, a slight smile on his face. *They must be feeling the pressure of declining cash flows*. ‘What did you do? Did you agree to his request?’

‘No. I didn’t. I told him to get lost.’

‘Jack, you have to be more diplomatic in these matters.’

‘Anton deserved what he got. He didn’t have proper authorisation. On top of that, he was bossing me around. Why should I be diplomatic with him?’

‘He must have been very annoyed.’

‘Yeah, he was very upset. He threatened me to keep my nose out of operational matters that didn’t concern me.’

‘Does his request hurt your surveillance?’

‘Of course, it does. If I switch off the circuit cameras covering five tables, a large part of the casino floor goes dark. Things can slip through our surveillance.’

‘Tell him so. Build a case why you can’t concede to his request. Tell him that you wish to cooperate, but five is too large a number. It makes you uncomfortable that such a large part of the floor goes dark. Be accommodative while still standing your ground.'

'But you said that you hadn't approved the increase in tables. Why then should I go sucking up to him?'

'You can't hide behind me. You must refuse him on operational grounds. Give him some slack. A little. Enough to keep him breathing. I know where he is coming from.'

Jack was quiet, trying to control his thoughts. But after a few seconds, he ended up asking, 'Boss, what is going on? Don't keep me in the dark! The only reason I am continuing in this casino is because of you.'

'Nothing is going on. You are reading too much into the situation.'

'Should I be looking out for a job? Please say something.'

'It's a good practice to be in the market, Jack.'

'Thank you! I would quit rather than report to Anton.'

'Who said anything about you reporting to anyone else? Don't be rash in your decision making. If you quit, what will happen to Nisha?'

'I will take her with me. I am not leaving her behind. The son of a bitch has been harassing her.'

'Why?'

'He tried to make a pass at her a few months back. She refused and he didn't like the rejection. He keeps pestering her to reconsider.'

'Oh my God! He really is getting out of hand.'

'Boss, that isn't all. Most of the time Anton is under the influence of cocaine. It makes him very aggressive. The other day, we caught a cheat and Anton beat him black and blue in the lower deck. The guy had cheated us of just a few thousand bucks. Have you seen his lockup down below? I fear that someday he is going to kill someone there.'

'Don't worry, Jack. While I am around here, no such thing will happen.'

'I trust you, boss. My worry is, how long are you around? With every passing day, Anton is becoming bolder and Bobby already behaves as if he owns this place.'

Jack left and Jayesh dialled the private detective agency he had hired to keep a tab on Anton's activities. 'Do you have any news for me?' he inquired.

'Not much except that his drug addiction has worsened. He now visits his dealer almost every other day.'

'Hmm! Keep a close watch on him.'

Where was the money coming from to pay for Anton's cocaine addiction? Jayesh wondered. In the past, Anton had pilfered money from the cash register on a few occasions. He had decided to look the other way, rewarding him for his loyalty. In retrospect, it was a mistake, one which emboldened Anton. But, of late, he had tightened the screws on the cash department, ensuring that such pilferage couldn't occur. Jayesh wondered if Bobby was aware of Anton's addiction. Would he stand by Anton when he fell? Anton was the weak link in this game of cat and mouse, the loose cannon. Jayesh had to keep up pressure on him and wait for him to crack or make a mistake.

THE FERRARI ON THE PORCH

Mirror, Mirror on the wall,
Who is the fairest of them all?

Once there had been no doubt about the answer. But life has moved on. Kumar Saurabh, however, was stuck in a time warp, imagining that he was still signing autographs for fans who could not have enough of him. It mattered little that his last blockbuster movie had released more than quarter a century earlier in 1989. This was followed by a row of flops in the early nineties that had ended his movie career. As time passed and the era of the Millennials gave way to Generation Z, his name was forgotten by the masses. So much so that he couldn't even manage an invite from *Grand Boss*, a reality television show where long forgotten celebrities desperately try to regain some fame for one last time. The only time he found himself in demand was during the elections. Political parties still called upon him to campaign for their candidates, making him stand for hours on end in an open jeep under the sweltering sun, waving at unsuspecting crowds. That too was now petering out. There was a time when he used to be the only one in the jeep, standing beside the candidate. He didn't need an introduction, the crowds flocked to see him, hold his hands. But now, he found himself amongst a group of B-grade celebrities, comics and dancers. Together as a group, they represented some value, but alone they were of little use. While these election campaigns were good for giving him a sense of importance, they didn't do much for the pocket.

Decades of high living and financial neglect had depleted his once overflowing coffers. Rubbing shoulders with List A celebrities, being seen around them was a very expensive proposition when there were no new films signed and not much money coming in. He had to pay a lot to be on the same invitation lists, dine at the same restaurants and play tennis at the same clubs as they did. Then he had to fork out a little more for the extras. These extras made all the difference. A restaurant manager running to greet him as he entered when a List A celebrity was dining at the restaurant made a world of a difference. This was essential to maintain his self-image. Every time he looked in the mirror, he knew that he was the fairest of them all; but he hasn't earned anything from endorsements or acting for over a decade and was surviving on investments he had made during his heyday. These were not enough to finance his extravagant lifestyle and he was on the verge of bankruptcy. Much of what he owned was already mortgaged with banks against loans that had financed his high-flying lifestyle during these years. Once the banks stopped lending, he borrowed money from friends and acquaintances. When the friends started avoiding him, he sought money from the unorganised sector.

The only valuable item still in his possession was his red 1959 Ferrari 250 GT Cabriolet. It was the love of his life. He drove it through the streets of South Mumbai, revving its engines at every traffic light. The car wasn't in mint condition, but still worth a few million dollars. He would park it deliberately on his porch for the whole world to admire it. It kept the creditors at bay. After all, none of them had lent him large sums of money. They all slept well at night dreaming about the red Ferrari that was parked on his porch. Why should he have any problem in paying their small sums! Fifty thousand dollars from one, a hundred from another, and so the list went on. What they didn't know was that the list ran almost into triple digits.

However, the fictitious life that he had nurtured and lived for so long was now on the verge of collapsing. He had recently been served a notice by one of his banks to pay up. Otherwise, they threatened to auction his house. He didn't have the money to pay up. It was only a matter of time before his dismal financial position became fodder for the gossip mills in the incestuous social circles of Mumbai. There was nothing to look forward to anymore, no purpose in his life. He had bitten anyone who had ever showered love on him, much like a rabid dog. His wife had died on him many years ago. He had driven her to suicide with his unfeeling, narcissistic behaviour. His only daughter had not spoken to him in years and didn't care whether he was dead or alive. The only people he expected to turn up at his funeral were his creditors.

He wasn't scared of death, but of facing reality. He feared facing his neighbours the day the news of his bankruptcy got out. He could imagine the hundreds of creditors who would line up outside his house. There was no turning back now. He knew what he needed to do. It was better to die like a king than live like a pauper. He knew once-famous film stars who had ended up in slums and died homeless on the street. He had no intention of being one of them.

There was one thing left to do before he put his grand plan into action. He had to make peace with his daughter. He opened the drawer beside his bed and pulled out the pistol and a loaded cartridge containing ten bullets and put them in his duffle bag. It was time to go to Goa, the state of sun and sand, one last time. He looked forward to playing at his favourite casino. They didn't know he was bankrupt. If he was going to die, he would die in style, make it a night to remember. He threw the duffle bag in the Ferrari, and the engine roared to life.

THE INTERVIEW

He didn't want to meet her. The inauguration of the new casino was only a few days away and a new controversy was the last thing he needed. She was making wild accusations. He wondered if someone was using her to take a piss at him behind his back. A front-page article attacking his establishment just when the new place was set for a grand opening would spoil everything. But that is exactly what she threatened to do.

'Either you clear the air and tell me your side of the story, or I will have to go ahead and print what I have gathered from my sources.'

Source based information had little factual basis. It usually relied on some cock and bull story that a journalist had heard over a bar counter, usually from a person who had more than his fair share of drinks. But that didn't make it any less damaging. And so, here he was, sitting in his office on a Saturday morning, reluctantly awaiting the journalist.

He would much rather be playing golf with his buddies. He looked at his watch again. Still 10 minutes to go, if she was on time. His eyes looked at the box of cigars on the table. He was tempted, but he controlled the urge to light one up. He didn't want to appear a pompous son of a bitch. At exactly 11 am, there was a knock on the door. She was a stickler for time. The door opened and he was surprised to see that she was much younger than he had imagined.

'Hello,' she said. 'I am Karishma.'

'Jayesh Shah,' he replied, standing up to shake her hand. He had to win her over. He had started on the wrong foot by avoiding her for the past week. It was time to make amends. He turned on his considerable charm. 'What would you like to drink?' he asked. 'It's very hot, perhaps a Margarita.'

'Thank you, but no,' she replied. 'I don't drink when I am working.'

'Oh! I am sorry. How about a Virgin Piña Colada in that case? My bartender does a twist on the original. The best you can have in Goa.'

She politely declined. 'A glass of iced water will be fine, Mr Shah.'

'Please call me Jayesh. I have read many of your articles. I am a big fan. I wasn't expecting to meet someone so young, given your accomplishments.'

'Thank you,' she replied.

'Let me apologise for not meeting you earlier, Karishma. I was busy with the preparations for the opening of our largest casino. I hope you didn't think I was avoiding you?'

'That thought did cross my mind, Jayesh,' she said, bluntly.

He realised that she would not be so easily won over. 'Well, in that case, let me not keep you waiting. As you will realise, I have nothing to hide.'

'Jayesh, did you get an opportunity to look at the questionnaire?'

'Yes, I did.'

'What did you think?'

'These are wild conjectures, Karishma. I don't know who your source is or what he has been smoking, but it isn't cigars. I can tell you that much.'

She smiled. Finally, he had broken the ice. 'So, you deny all the accusations?'

'Absolutely. I have built this establishment from scratch. I will not allow a competitor to malign its reputation without basis.'

'So, no money laundering happens here? No mafia money is involved in financing your activities? No prostitution rackets?'

'Ha-ha! Someone has been reading a lot of James Hadley Chase lately. This is not the 1930s Chicago. We are in the new millennium. I run a licensed entertainment business. Everything is above board. We pay our taxes regularly.'

'Last I heard, beating up people was not considered above board.'

'Excuse me! What do you mean?' he exclaimed, dropping the pen on the table. *That Anton was becoming a liability and needed to be reined in.*

'I am talking about people beaten black and blue being found regularly on the beach. They found one last week too.'

'What's that got to do with us? I haven't seen any police complaint filed against us. Tell me if I am wrong?'

'They are too scared to file anything with the police.'

'You can't blame us for every drunken brawl on the beach,' he said. And before, she could ask any more questions, he smiled gently and said, 'I wonder, if your tip was anonymous? Someone has sent you on a wild goose chase'.

She tried her best to hide her expression, but the poker player sitting across the table was very astute. He knew that he had hit a raw nerve. He suspected that she didn't have concrete evidence and was shooting in the dark. He smiled, satisfied that he had put her on back foot. It was time to light that victory cigar. But Jayesh had underestimated her. She was ready with a counter offensive and the gloves were off now.

'Who is the real owner of this casino?' she asked.

Ouch! He hadn't seen that one coming. She packed more punch than he had envisaged. He put the cigar back in the box and replied calmly, 'I am.' But he wasn't smiling any more.

'There are rumours doing the round that a politician owns this establishment,' she said.

'Ha-ha! That's a first,' he replied, smiling again. 'Only a week earlier I heard a politician asking for casinos to be burned down.'

'You don't really believe all these pre-poll rhetorics, do you?' she said. 'A casino is the perfect front to launder black money.'

'I have nothing to add. You have stumped me by raising this question about the ownership. Why don't you go and check the records?'

'I already did,' she replied.

'Well, why don't you tell me what you found?'

'As per the records, you are the owner.'

'Thank God!' he said sarcastically. 'You had me worried for a bit.'

'But I am interested in the beneficial ownership.'

'Karishma, you are again conjecturing. I don't like the direction in which this interview is heading.'

'Then, why do you sound so edgy?' she asked.

'Am I not supposed to be edgy? I have a journalist raising doubts about the ownership of an establishment that I have built with my sweat and tears and considered my own till a few minutes back.'

'Yeah! But according to you I am merely conjecturing. Then why this fear?'

'The fact that you are willing to explore this lead is reason enough for me to be fearful. It is election season after all. I am a simple businessman. Business and politics don't mix well. Frankly, I am beginning to doubt if this interview is about me or my casino at all.'

She smiled. 'You are an intelligent man.'

'I am only a pawn, collateral damage, am I not? There are larger forces at play here.' He looked at her questioningly.

She didn't reply.

'Actually, I am curious. Did your source also mention a name?'

'Why is that relevant?'

'It might give me some clue about who is behind this.'

'I can't say that I have a name at this moment,' she replied.

But he knew that she did. She already had a name and given her line of questioning it was that of his benefactor. He was still wondering what to ask her next, when she suddenly stood up from her seat.

'I better be leaving now.'

'You are leaving?' he asked, a little surprised. 'Have I cleared your doubts?'

'I didn't say that.'

'Please don't leave this sword hanging over my head,' he pretended to plead. 'I hope you keep me in the loop before you print something.'

'Don't worry. This enquiry isn't over yet,' she said. 'There are many questions that still need answering. By the way, when is this great inauguration?'

Aha! Was she angling for an invite? Actually, it may not be a bad idea, Jayesh thought. 'Very soon,' he replied. 'In fact, I was finalising the invitation list and your name is right at the top.'

She smiled.

'I don't like page three events, Jayesh. But I will take up your offer. Maybe I will find a new story to write about?'

'I hope the event will shed more light on our business and help in clearing the air. You will get to see what we actually do.'

As soon as Karishma left, Jayesh called Bobby to his chamber and then dialled Pankaj Adhikari on the speaker phone. 'Boss, I have Bobby with me. We need to speak urgently.'

'What is it now?' asked Pankaj Adhikari. 'Why can't you two sort out your differences like adults and keep me out of it?'

'It's not about us. It is about you.'

'What?'

'I gave an interview to a newspaper a few minutes back. The journalist was asking questions about the ownership of this casino.'

'What? Why wasn't I informed earlier?'

'She sent me a questionnaire last week. But all it had were mundane questions. Nothing we hadn't handled before. I didn't think it fit to involve you. But she stumped me today.'

'Maybe she is just trying to stir something to see what happens?'

'Boss, I don't think so. I feel that someone has tipped her off.'

'There is no honour among thieves anymore,' said Pankaj Adhikari.

'Who do you suspect?' asked Jayesh.

'The opposition, who else? There was a code: never turn against our own. We gave loud speeches abusing each other, but come evening, we drank from the same bottle of whiskey. What is this world coming to?'

There was a moment of silence.

'Did she mention my name?'

'She didn't. But I am pretty sure she has you in mind.'

'Hmm! Bobby, what do you think we should do?'

'Boss, we could pay her off. Stop this investigation in its tracks.'

'We shouldn't,' said Jayesh. 'She doesn't come across as someone who can be bribed. Also, if we offer her money, we will confirm her hunch that she is on the right path.'

'Hmm! Why don't we pay the newspaper instead, advertise with them and cajole them into dropping the investigation?' suggested Bobby.

'They are crowdfunded,' replied Jayesh. 'But it is worth a try.'

'Let Bobby take care of it. You concentrate on the inauguration,' said Pankaj Adhikari.

'As you say, boss.'

'Bobby, what if it doesn't work and they continue with the investigation?'

'Boss, perhaps a tragic accident. A dozen people die every week on the roads. Another one will make no difference.'

'It is a risky proposition. It will create a wave of sympathy and awaken every vigilante in the state. We should instead create noise, enough noise to confuse the public.'

'Boss, I don't follow you?'

'Pay a few journalists and get similar stories printed against the opposition. Launch a smear campaign against them. The investigation will be lost in the noise.'

YOU HAVE BEEN PLAYED

Anton walked into Bobby's chamber with a light heart. Until that morning, he had been wondering how to save face in front of Bobby. A few days earlier, Jack had absolutely refused to increase the number of operational tables without proper authorisation. He had tried to convince him in all kinds of ways to no avail. Then out of the blue this morning, Jack had come to him in a conciliatory mood. Fleetingly, Anton wondered who or what had made him change his mind. But he was so relieved that he would be able to keep his word to Bobby that he gave it no further thought.

'Boss, I have done it,' he said, triumphantly. 'I told you I will manage it.'

'What have you managed to do, Anton?' asked Bobby.

'I have managed to increase the number of operating tables.'

'Oh! That is great news, indeed. We are one step closer to our goal. By the way, how many operating tables do we have now?'

'We now have three operating tables in each of the casinos, a total of nine.'

'Is that all?' said Bobby, looking disappointed. 'All that boastful talk, and all you could manage was a measly three tables per casino. I was expecting more, Anton. I thought the least you would manage was to double the number of operating tables.'

'So did I, boss. Actually, I wanted to do even better than that number and have five operating tables per casino.'

'Why didn't you?'

'Well, I have to inform Jack before we can operate these tables. You know, he handles the electronic surveillance. We can't operate these tables unless the relevant cameras are switched off.'

'What did Jack say?'

'Jack refused point-blank to entertain my request. He said he won't do it.'

'Son of a bitch. Why did he refuse?'

'He didn't give me a reason. Told me to get lost. He doesn't need a reason to play ball. He doesn't report to me.'

'Anton, lets remain focussed. You have already made your point about his reporting earlier. I heard you last time. Let's not go there. But you say there has been an increase in the number of operating tables. How did you manage it?'

'I stood my ground, and kept putting pressure on him. I told him to keep his nose out of matters that didn't concern him.'

'He agreed? Like that?'

'Yeah! I guess good sense prevailed over him. He met me this morning and begged my forgiveness.'

Bobby stared at Anton with an expression of disbelief. 'That is a little hard to digest,' he said. 'Tell me, Anton, what exactly happened. This is important.'

'Boss, I am serious. He came to me in the morning and said that he wanted to cooperate, that after all, we are on the same side. He wanted to support the business operation. But, turning off five cameras was too risky, as a large part of the casino floor would go dark. Yet, given the business need, he was willing to turn off three cameras.'

'Hmm! That sounds more plausible. You agreed?'

'What choice did I have? It was three tables or status quo.'

Bobby nodded.

'Anton, you have been played. It wasn't Jack, it was Jayesh who agreed to your request.'

'Huh? What do you mean?'

'Three tables, while better than the status quo, is not enough for us to meet our numbers. Jayesh knows that. He is keeping a tight leash, while pretending to cooperate with us. Otherwise, this would have been an opportunity to complain about him to the Boss. But, I can no longer do so, as you have accepted their offer. We need to do more, Anton.'

Anton realised that he had been taken for a ride and was angry. 'Let me increase the operating tables to five tomorrow. Let's see what happens.' he said belligerently.

'You will do no such thing. This is exactly what Jayesh wants us to do. He is trying to prove that we are irresponsible and careless. After Jack's well thought out response, we have no option but to play along. We have already made one mistake with the tickets, we cannot give Jayesh another opportunity to make us look like fools.'

'What should we do?'

'The only workable way to improve our cash flow is to increase our lending operations.'

Anton smiled with relief. 'Finally, a product which is under our control and for which we don't need anyone's permission. Boss, what are we waiting for? Let's open the flood gates.'

'Not so fast. I am not conversant with the credit profile of our customers. We need to handle this carefully. Otherwise, we risk running into bad debts.'

'Don't you worry. I know our customers like the back of my hands. I will help you carry out their credit appraisal.'

A TIME TO MOVE ON

A mosque, a Hindu temple and a Buddhist temple sit side by side on a single street in downtown Singapore. They reflect the multicultural ethnicity of the city state—Chinese (76%), Malay (15%) and Tamil Indians (7.5%). At the end of the street lies the Maxwell Hawker Centre, popular amongst locals and tourists alike for its affordable yet delicious street food. Jack's father ran a small stall selling Hainanese Chicken Rice at the Hawker Centre. They were a lower middle-class Chinese family and life was not easy. His father started early, at 4:30 am, and was back home only late at night. Jack seldom saw his father, except on Sundays, when he would return early to have dinner with the family. His mother worked hard too, preparing breakfast, seeing him off to school and then finishing the household chores. Once these were done, she left for the Hawker Centre to assist her husband in serving the queues of hungry customers that thronged the stall. Jack's father was proud of his profession, which provided their livelihood. But he didn't want his only son to follow his path. So, Jack's requests to assist him at the Hawker Centre were always denied. 'I work hard, so that someday my son can wear a tie around his neck.' The hard but honest life had inculcated the strong value system in Jack. That value system was now pricking his conscience.

'Darling, are you ok?' asked a soft voice.

Jack and Nisha were dining at a seaside restaurant in South Goa. They hadn't met outside of work for a long time since Jack had been extremely busy testing the surveillance system for the new casino. This was meant to be a long overdue romantic dinner. Nisha had played her part by dressing up for the evening in a sexy black halter gown with a deep neck, accentuating her curves. She had the attention of every man at the restaurant, except the one sitting opposite her. Jack was lost in his own world, dressed down in a pair of jeans and a Polo T-shirt. The soft voice penetrated his thoughts and emerging from them, he replied, 'Yeah, yeah, I am fine.'

'No. You are not. You are physically sitting next to me, but your mind is elsewhere.'

'Darling, I am sorry. I didn't realise it was so apparent.'

'It is. I didn't say anything when your soup went cold. But you are still lost. Tell me, what is bothering you?'

'I don't know where to start. A lot of things are playing on my mind. For starters, Anton.'

'Isn't he always! Why do you let him get to you? If only you thought of me as often as you think of him, all would be hunky dory. Tell me what's happened this time?'

'Two days ago, he asked me, actually it was more like he ordered me to shut down a few surveillance cameras.'

'I presume you declined.'

'Of course, I did. I politely told him to fuck off.'

'Ha-ha! Politeness redefined.'

'Nisha, he was ordering me around. What did you expect me to do? You know how I feel about this hanky-panky stuff they do at the casino. Anyway, I declined and he created a big ruckus.'

'That's not surprising.'

'Are you sympathising with him?'

'Not at all. He has a big ego and his behaviour is predictable'

'He created such a stink, that I thought it better to play safe and run the matter by boss.'

'Hmm! That's smart.'

'Well! Here comes the shocker. Boss asked me to accommodate him.'

'Accommodate him? Oops! That must have hurt.'

'Yeah! Anton laughed on my face. I can still see his grinning face every time I close my eyes.'

'What? Darling, do I now have to compete with him even in your dreams? Get over him. Sooner or later, he will give you an opportunity to return the favour with interest.'

'Of that, I am certain. He always does. But there is something else.'

'Come out with it all,' said Nisha. 'I can't bear this mood of yours anymore.'

'I asked Boss if I should be looking out for a job. He didn't even bat an eyelid and told me that it was a good idea.'

'What else did you expect, cornering him like that? Given the changing circumstances his reply is absolutely right.'

'I guess so. I don't know why I was hoping for some comfort.'

'Darling, if you wanted comfort, you should have come to me,' said Nisha, holding his hands and smiling.

Jack looked up and smiled. 'You know, sweetheart, I have been thinking for a while now that we should look for a new job. My discussions with boss have only reaffirmed my resolve.'

'Ok. What do you have in mind? We are already employed with the largest player in the country.'

'Exactly! The Indian market is too damn small. We have to evaluate opportunities outside India.'

'Outside India?' Nisha was surprised.

'Yeah! Like Singapore. It's my home so it will be easier for us to settle down there.'

'Woah! That's a new idea! Don't get me wrong, I am excited. But I hope you have thought this through.'

'Don't worry. I have it all figured out. I am just waiting for this inauguration to be done. I intend to put in my papers.'

'You will do what? Darling, don't make any hasty decisions. Have you found a new job?'

'There's this casino operator who has been pursuing me for a while. He made me an offer a few months back. I was dilly dallying. I called him yesterday to ask if the offer was still open. He asked me when I could join.'

'Hmm! What about me? Do you think I can find a job in Singapore?'

'Of course, you will. I have spoken to this employer about you and told them about your superior skills and your experience.'

'My superior skills?'

They both laughed aloud.

'I told them that I don't work alone. I have an eye on the floor that I trust, and that you and I work as a team. They are very keen to meet you.'

'I am impressed. You seem to have it all covered.'

'Almost everything. We still need to work on your taste buds. Get you to like Hainanese Chicken Rice.'

He squeezed her fingers gently and smiled.

'So, do I have your permission?'

Nisha leaned forward and gave him a deep passionate kiss.

'Of course, you do. You didn't think that I was going to let you go on your own, did you? I am excited.'

'Don't you need to ask your father?'

'Ask him? Not at all. You know my relationship with him. We haven't spoken for a long time.'

Jack held both her hands as he looked into her eyes. 'Darling, I think you should meet him before you leave and close this chapter in your life. You have carried this baggage for far too long.'

Nisha bit on her upper lip as she looked down at the table.

'I know this is difficult for you, sweetie,' said Jack, still holding her hands. 'I will always be there for you.'

She raised her head and looked at him. 'He is coming to Goa for the opening of the Sultan. He has been calling me, he wants to meet me. I have been avoiding him. But now, I think I shall meet him. I cannot guarantee anything, Jack. I have very deep anger and resentment against him. But I promise that I will try.'

'Thank you, darling. I can't ask for anything more.' Jack leaned forward and gave her a peck on her cheek. She smiled.

'What about you, Jack?' she asked. 'Have you told your parents?'

'Not yet. I will tell them tomorrow, now that you have approved of the plan.'

'They will be thrilled. Their only son returning home.'

'Yeah! They will be very excited. My mother might even shed a few tears of joy. But my father will not show his emotions. He likes to act tough.'

'Does he still work at the Hawker Centre?'

'Yes, he does.'

'Why doesn't he retire? Surely, you can support him.'

'Oh! You think I haven't tried? He refuses to take a penny from me. Instead, he keeps reminding me that the Chicken Rice has paid for my education.'

'Ha-ha! He acts tough, but he loves you, Jack. You must be proud of him.'

'I am very proud of him. He works hard and lives an honest life. I wish I could be as forthright as him.'

'Baby, why do you say that? Please don't do this to yourself. You are a good man.'

'Am I? Do I do an honest job?'

'Of course, you do. Why do you doubt yourself? You do your job with integrity. It is an honourable job, to catch cheats and fraudsters.'

'Don't be so naïve, Nisha. We keep our eyes shut, but that doesn't absolve us of what happens at the casino. Why do I need to switch-off the surveillance? Don't I know what's going on?'

Nisha was quiet.

'It is time to move out.'

A BLESSING IN DISGUISE

Anton and Bobby perused through the list of high-rollers who would be attending the opening of the new casino. Bobby was under tremendous pressure, snapping at Anton every now and then. He felt sandwiched between an aggressive Pankaj Adhikari on one side and a shrewd Jayesh Shah on the other. Pankaj Adhikari called him almost every day demanding larger sums of money to fund the election expenditure. And Jayesh was keeping a tight control on the casino operations, limiting his options to launder money. With restrictions already in place on the number of operating tables and the tickets, Bobby had little choice but to lend larger sums of money to the high-rollers. But this mode was fraught with credit risk.

'Mrs Dhillon. What's her story?' asked Bobby.

'Tanya Dhillon is the wife of a rich industrialist from Ludhiana.'

'I have never seen her husband at the casino.'

'Neither has anyone else,' replied Anton. 'But I have often seen her cosying up to Kumar Saurabh.'

'I am not interested in her love life. Tell me, will she pay up?'

'She is safe. You can lend her a million dollars without any sweat. If she doesn't pay up, her husband will. After all, prestige is everything in a business family.'

'Can we lend her more?'

'No, you cannot. She is very meticulous. She comes here to win, not to enjoy. She will play only when the odds favour her.'

'You mean to say that just because she has more money at her disposal, doesn't mean that she is going to play.'

'Exactly.'

'Ok. What about Kumar Saurabh?'

Anton's eyes lit up in excitement.

'He is a gambler at heart, betting on everything from the toss of a coin, to a game of cricket. Throw him an odd and Kumar will wager on it.'

'What work does he do?'

'He used to be a Bollywood actor. Was a big star in the nineties.'

'How are his finances now?'

'I don't know. But he is a regular at our casino. He has never defaulted in the past.'

'How much money can he take?'

'As much as you will lend him. But, treat him with caution, because when he is in his element, he can create havoc.'

'Anton, this is not going anywhere,' said Bobby. 'The ones that I want to lend to don't want my money, and those that I don't want to lend to because they might not return what is mine want it all.'

'Boss, you want borrowers with both the ability and the intention to repay. That is the ideal case scenario. It seldom exists in real life.'

'We have to be careful.'

'Being careful is good. But, being too careful is bad for business.'

'What do you suggest?'

'In my opinion, we should lay more emphasis on their past payment history. That one metric captures everything.'

'It's not that simple, Anton. You don't have a clue about the source of funds.'

'You are right. I don't care, so long as the guy is paying up. Ability is based on circumstances, but intention is a function of character. I lay more emphasis on the person's intention to pay.'

'Even if I were to agree with you, we still need more borrowers.'

'We haven't yet considered Balwant. He and his friends would easily take another two million.'

'How do you know he even needs the money? He hasn't called us yet.'

'He always does. He already owes us a million and a half from last week.'

'What? And you think he is good for more?'

'Boss, Balwant has lost tens of millions of dollars over the past two years at the casino. His friends have lost even more.'

'But that was in the past.'

'Boss, this argument can go on for ever. I will take a quick round of the floor and come back.'

Bobby began to pace up and down, mulling over the discussion. He was gradually coming to accept Anton's point of view. He still didn't completely agree with what Anton had to say, but there was wisdom in his words. He felt more comfortable now; the morning edginess had disappeared. Zero risk was a theoretical concept with little relevance in real life. A lending operation could never be without risk. One had to compare the expected benefits with the anticipated level of risk. So long as the benefits exceeded the risk, one was good to go. Any attempt to minimise the risk beyond a level would be at the cost of the business.

He was still thinking about this when Balwant called. He picked up the receiver with anticipation, knowing how important this call was. It would decide whether he would meet his numbers. He decided to approach the subject with an open mind, but what he heard blew his mind away.

'I need a credit of five million dollars for the night,' said Balwant, in a calm voice. 'Two million for myself and three million for my friends.'

'Give me a minute,' said Bobby, a little disoriented, trying hard to absorb the seven-digit number that Balwant had thrown at him. This number was completely out of whack, nowhere near the million or two that he had been working with. He was quite sure that the casino had never taken such a large wager on a single customer before, and for good reason. He also remembered that Balwant had an outstanding of a million and half dollars against his name.

'Balwant, you have never taken such a large sum of money in the past,' he said.

'I am feeling lucky, Bobby. There is nothing else to say,' Balwant replied nonchalantly. The casinos had spoilt him, always agreeing to every request he had made in the past. He was not used to answering questions. Bobby was walking on thin ice.

Son of a bitch! Easy for you to say that, thought Bobby. 'But you already have a million and half outstanding from earlier,' he said.

'Maybe I do. Listen Bobby, why don't you do your homework and call me back. But know this: either you give me the money I have asked for, or you lose my business. No half deals this time. Last I checked, there were many casinos in town vying for my business.'

Bobby tried to calm him down, reminding him of their past relationship built on mutual trust. But Balwant was in no mood to listen and cut him short midway. 'One more thing,' he said. 'When I play that night, I want Ruby by my side. Once I have stopped playing, she goes back with me to the hotel. Too long have you guys been putting me off on some pretext. No excuses this time.'

This conversation was going horribly wrong. Bobby wanted to cajole Balwant, but before he could find the right words to say, the line went dead. He cussed loudly in frustration; wiping sweat from his forehead. He was still wondering what to do next when Anton walked in.

'Boss, what happened?' Anton asked. 'You are looking all worked up.'

Bobby told him.

'Five million dollars!' said Anton excitedly. 'This is great news. It will sort out all our problems.'

'But, don't you see the risk in lending such a large sum to him?'

'Boss, this is a blessing in disguise. What are you talking about? See his past payment history. He always pays up. Sometimes there is a delay of a week or two, but he eventually pays up. The guys in the collection department swear by him.'

'I am not comfortable with this.'

'If it makes you feel any better, Balwant is about to come into big money.'

'How do you know?'

'One of the dealers overheard him telling Ruby about some land parcel which he was about to sell.'

'It could be only talk.'

'In any case, you have nothing to worry about. With Ruby by his side, he doesn't stand a chance. You know Ruby is bad luck.'

'Shouldn't we run it by Jayesh once?'

'Boss, are you joking? If we close this deal, we will meet our numbers. Jayesh is a vested party. Why would you seek his advice? Think what advice you would have given had you been in his place.'

Bobby listened to Anton, but he was uneasy. This did not feel quite right.

'Such opportunities come seldom. You must seize the moment. If you do, the throne will be yours. If you don't, you alone will be responsible for the outcome.'

'By the way, what is this about Ruby not being allowed to do a night out with him?'

'Ha-ha! Did this issue also crop up in the discussion? We don't allow any customer to take Ruby back to the hotel to protect her identity.'

'Are you telling me that Balwant doesn't know about her?'

'I don't think he does. Otherwise, he would not have asked for this favour.'

'What should we do?'

'We don't have a choice, do we? Let him have what he desires so much. We have protected her for far too long.'

THE THREE VICES

Balwant belonged to the farming community that lived in the villages surrounding the urban towns of Gurgaon, Faridabad and Sonepat in North India. He had fond memories of his childhood, of running through fields of mustard with his hands stretched out wide, the wind blowing against his face, his mind free of even an iota of worry.

But it was now a distant dream. With the onset of the real estate boom, almost everything had changed overnight in his village. The lush green and yellow landscape were now barren. In its place stood concrete structures in varying degrees of completion, trying hard to meet the insatiable demand of a burgeoning urban middle class. Advertising hoardings promised Venice, the French Riviera and other fancy themes to gullible home buyers who all wanted to fulfil their dream of owning a house.

The simple farmers were coerced through all possible means to sacrifice their ancestral land holdings in favour of hungry real estate developers. They came in open jeeps filled with sacks of money, armed with the relevant property papers and inkpads, moving from one house to the next, one village at a time. Deals were struck in minutes, before you knew it someone was pressing your fingers against the ink pad and dolling out cash. They weren't discreet; on the contrary they made sure that they were loud, especially when they were handing out wads of cash. The poor farmers who had thus far lived a simple and frugal life, just managing to make ends meet, didn't stand a chance against this aggressive onslaught. They were saddled with more cash than they could imagine, and much more than they could count. The entire community was transformed into multi-millionaires overnight.

As the story of their newfound riches spread across the country, all kinds of people turned up at these villages, trying to lighten the financial load of the poor farmers. The first to arrive were the bankers, but they failed in their effort to find new customers. They had the herculean task of teaching saving habits to people who seldom had the money to eat two proper meals in a day.

While saving as a theme didn't appeal to the farming folk, consumption came naturally to them. All their lives they had struggled with money, forced to make hard choices. Suddenly, they had all the money in the world to fulfil both their needs and desires. In a bid to outdo their neighbours and show off their newly acquired status in the village community, the farmers went on a spending spree. Every item of consumption became a necessity, driven more by the desire to show off than actual need.

Balwant remembered the day the first mud house was pulled down in his neighbourhood. The mud houses had served them so well for decades, keeping them cool in the sweltering heat of the summers. Now they became a sign of old-fashioned poverty. His own mother went on a *dharna* (protest), demanding a new, big concrete house, refusing to eat food, nagging his father into submission.

The bulky concrete structure that replaced it was more in keeping with the times, but baked under the afternoon sun, requiring constant air conditioning to keep it cool. When a neighbour bought a Mahindra Scorpio to replace his bullock cart, Balwant's father didn't sleep for many nights. After all, an owner's pride was the neighbour's envy. His father's insomnia ended only when he bought an even larger SUV. But the glory was short lived, as within a few weeks someone outdid him by buying a still larger and more expensive vehicle. This one up-man-ship continued unabated, so what if the village cried for proper roads and there were few trained drivers to drive these vehicles. Similarly, white goods like televisions, refrigerators, and washing machines entered households which didn't have regular electricity supply. Family celebrations like weddings became grand affairs where money was splurged like water. The expenses continued, but the money refused to get over.

It was almost a year later that the first casino agents arrived at this lavish banquet. By this time, no item of luxury had escaped the villagers. The excesses were visible everywhere. Where there was a single Scorpio earlier, Pajero and Land cruisers stood now. Rolexes adorned the hands of the old *kakas* (Uncles) who still smoked *hookah* (Shisha). The casino agents went to work quickly, before the villagers ran out of money. Within a fortnight, a junket to Goa was organised for the influencers in these villages. They were given free air tickets; hotel stay and anything else they desired to get them there. There was no escape for the poor villagers whose only source of entertainment thus far had been the dilapidated cinema halls, the odd *mujra* (Dance) at a family wedding or the annual circus. They found themselves in the grip of the three vices which have plagued both men and gods alike from time immemorial: gambling, alcohol and women.

Where Gods had fallen, what chance did poor, mortal men have? They were simply overwhelmed. The concoction of the three vices was so corrosive that it dissolved the fabric of conscience, exposing threadbare the basic instincts that underlie every human being. Some were seduced by the thrill of gambling, some by the free-flowing alcohol, and others by the women.

The elders returned to the village and narrated tales about a paradise on earth. Goa became the only topic of conversation among the men who sat in closed huddles smoking their *hookahs* and listening to unbelievable tales of money and wine and women told excitedly by their comrades. Soon, the stories spread like a wild fire through the entire farming community in the region. But, what the visitors to Goa forgot to tell their fellow villagers was the amount of money they lost at the casino. It was a forgivable oversight, as money held little value in the lives of the village folk at that time.

The effect of such viral marketing was immediately visible. The next weekend another fifty villagers made the trip to the paradise on earth. The number increased to a hundred in the week thereafter. In just a few months, thousands were visiting Goa to play at its casinos. Within a year, gambling, alcoholism and prostitution had taken its toll on the entire farming community. The farmers found their cash dwindling, and they were no longer in possession of their ancestral land which had been their only source of livelihood. Economic turmoil strained social relationships, leading to depression and suicides, and a wave of crime gripped the entire region.

Balwant had seen it all, lives being destroyed in front of his own eyes. He knew the right path, but the rush of gambling was so addictive that he was helpless, much like the other village folks before him.

YOU ARE A BETTER PERSON THAN I WAS

Nisha arrived at the coffee shop 10 minutes early, singing her favourite song, excited about starting a new life with Jack in Singapore. She sat at a table in the far end of the coffee shop, away from the crowds and ordered a skimmed latte. She was here to meet her father. It was only on Jack's advice that she had agreed to see him; otherwise, she found it hard to get over her anger at the way he had treated her and her mother. She had not spoken to him in many years. Although he had made several attempts to talk with her at the casino, she had always completely ignored him. However, she felt obliged to tell him that she planned to leave the country. Their relationship wasn't cordial, but, after all, he was the only family she had. She was still mulling over what to say when she heard the loud growl of the Ferrari outside.

'Trust him to make a grand entrance,' she muttered. 'He is so full of himself.'

There was a commotion at the door, but she ignored it, looking at her Instagram instead. People ran to admire the red Ferrari and take selfies with the car.

'No one remembers him', she said to herself. 'All they are interested in is his car.'

But then an old aunty got up and ran towards her father, hugging him and asking for a selfie. That attracted everyone's attention and people realised that a star, albeit a rather faded one, was amongst them. Only then was Kumar Saurabh swarmed by fans. It didn't matter that most of them didn't know who he was. They could always find out later. For now, they kept him busy signing autographs and posing for photographs.

Oh my God! Now I will have to deal with his bloated ego, thought Nisha in dismay.

'Hello there,' he said, waving at her.

She had nowhere else to look, but she pretended to be looking elsewhere.

'Thank you for meeting me,' he said, pulling up a chair next to her.

'You didn't leave me with a choice,' she replied. 'You have been hounding me for the past week. Why this new-found love for your daughter?'

'I needed to discuss something important with you.'

'Hah! Just as I thought. Why does it always have to be about you?' she asked.

'Please don't say that.'

'Why not?'

'Ok. In that case, you tell me. Tell me what's happening in your life?'

'Sure! I am going to leave this country soon.'

She was amused to see the shock on his face.

'What? Where are you going? When are you leaving?'

'Singapore. I am going to make a fresh start. It is getting boring here. We plan to leave in a fortnight.'

'We? Who is "we"? Have you thought through this?'

'Oh! So, you are concerned? Have you suddenly woken up to your fatherly duties?'

'Young lady, don't be so condescending. You brought this topic up. At least tell me his name?'

'His name is Jack. We are colleagues. I have known him for a few years. If it gives you any comfort, he is nothing like you.'

'Well, I guess congratulations are in order. I wish you both a bright future.'

'Thank you. Now tell me why you wanted to meet me?'

'I don't know how to put it, I guess there is no gentle way of saying this—I am on the verge of bankruptcy.'

'Bankruptcy? How did you manage that?'

'It is a long story. The only valuable asset still in my possession is my Ferrari. I would like you to have it.'

Nisha looked at him in silence, visibly shocked. She knew that the Ferrari meant everything to him.

'I know, I haven't been an ideal father,' he continued. 'I can't change the past, but I can make amends for the future.'

Was he trying to bribe his way to her heart? She remembered what Jack had said and tried her best to control her anger, but couldn't.

'You woke up this morning feeling guilty, and you thought you could buy my forgiveness. Is that what this is all about?'

'No. Perhaps, I didn't say it right. You are getting me wrong.'

But it was too late, she had lost her temper. She cut him off mid-sentence. 'Wait!' she yelled, as the entire coffee shop looked curiously at them. 'I am not finished yet. First, you were a terrible husband, then a bad father. You drove my mother to suicide. You scarred my childhood forever. No sir, you can't walk in and out of my life as per your whims and fancies. I have suffered miserably because of you.'

'I am really sorry,' he begged. 'I have no defence for my past behaviour. Please forgive me, Nisha.'

'I never realised how much I hated you. Please leave, sir. Please leave me alone.'

His attempts to hug her were futile. As he stood up to leave, he pushed the car keys towards her.

'I will not accept that,' she yelled. 'Take it back.'

'Darling, think straight,' he begged. 'I know you are angry.'

'Don't pretend to understand how I feel at this moment. You have no idea. Just go.'

Kumar Saurabh left the coffee shop. Nisha sat there fuming and blankly looking at her phone. She kept playing the conversation in her mind. As she calmed down, she slowly realised that she had behaved terribly with her father. She had allowed all the old anger and resentment to overcome her and had paid no attention to what he was trying to say. She picked up her phone and dialled Jack.

'I am sorry, darling,' she said, the tears now spilling down her face. 'I tried my best to be rational, but I couldn't control my emotions. I completely lost it.'

'Don't cry, sweetheart,' he replied. 'You tried, and that is what counts.'

But Nisha was upset and agitated all day. Finally, later that evening, she made up her mind. Before she left for the casino, she picked up her phone and dialled her father.

Kumar Saurabh was delighted to see her name on the screen of his phone.

'I am sorry about this morning,' she said.

He listened silently.

'It is wrong of me to hold such resentments for so long. I want you to know that I have forgiven you,' she continued.

'Thank you,' Kumar Saurabh said warmly. 'You are a better person than I ever was, Nisha'

Before he could say anymore, the phone was disconnected.

Nisha slept like a baby that night. She didn't know it, but she had just relieved her father of huge burden. Kumar Saurabh partied till the early hours of the morning.

THE STARS HAVE ALIGNED FOR A TAKEOVER

Ruby was in her room listening to the chatter of half a dozen girls from the escort service. They were exchanging notes, gossiping and giggling about their clients. The atmosphere was relaxed and Ruby softly whistled the tune of the latest dance number. She liked these quiet times when the girls were relaxed and she learnt about their problems and concerns and shared their laughter.

The door opened; a girl ran in saying that Anton was on his way. A chill descended in the room, the laughter was silenced and the girls quickly got up and left. No one wanted to meet Anton. He never failed to remind them who they were, making them feel small about themselves, abusing and calling them names as he moved his slimy hands all over their bodies.

Ruby waited for Anton. She didn't have the luxury of walking away. She had to face him and bear his spite, though it wasn't always a one-way street. At every opportunity, she gave it back to him with interest. The door opened and Anton entered the room with a smirk on his face, which Ruby knew only too well.

'Hello darling,' he said, sarcastically. 'Looking rather relaxed, did you just jerk off?'

'Fuck off,' she replied. 'At least be creative, your jokes are stale.'

'Oh! How I wish I was creative, baby, but luckily for you, I am not into those kinds of things.'

'Cut the bullshit. What is it that you want?'

'No small talk, baby? Ok, if that's the way you want it. You are to escort Balwant at the launch.'

'So, what's new?'

'The drunk is playing the largest wager of his life and wants his *Laila* by his side.'

She shook her head in disbelief. For the past two years, Balwant had been losing money almost every time she was his escort, and yet he had asked for her when he had so much at stake. It didn't make sense.

'I won't do it,' she replied. 'I don't want it on my conscience.'

'Ha! A whore with a conscience. You surprise me. Don't tell me you have a soft spot for that Villager! Laila and Majnu, huh? What a pair!' Anton laughed uproariously.

'How can you guys do it? Suck him dry of every last drop of blood in his body!'

'Why so much melodrama, darling? A whore fucks. She doesn't ask whom she fucks.'

Ruby kept quiet, simmering with anger.

'By the way, you will be needing this,' said Anton, holding out her passport.

Ruby looked at him in surprise. 'You trust me with my passport?'

'I wouldn't even trust your type with a massage,' he said. 'But, it's your lucky night. The drunk insists on taking you to his hotel.'

'What!' she said, shocked.

'Yeah! You heard me. It will be one hell of a romping night,' he said, rubbing it in.

'Please don't do this,' she begged. 'He doesn't know who I am.'

'Yeah! I can only imagine the look on his face when you show him that you are a bigger man than he is,' Anton laughed. 'I guess I should be asking who will be romping whom?'

Ruby pushed aside the chair and stood up to leave.

'I am not finished here,' he said, angrily. 'Where do you think you are going?'

'I am going to my boss. I don't take my orders from you.'

'Bitch, you better get used to taking orders from me. Don't you see the writing on the wall?'

Ruby stormed out of the room, followed by Anton in close pursuit. She pushed open the door to Jayesh's room and barged in.

'Yes, I have looked at the list you sent. It seems fine, but add some more wines; good ones, mind you…' Jayesh was saying on the phone. He looked up in surprise at Ruby.

'You can't do this to me,' she shouted. 'You both promised that you will protect my identity at all costs.'

'What's the big deal?' said Anton, walking in behind her. 'You are who you are.'

'I am proud to be a ladyboy,' she replied. 'But, in this instance, you told me to play a woman and keep my identity a secret.'

Jayesh glanced at them, said, 'Okay, that's done then,' into the phone, put it gently down and looked up. He read the situation immediately.

'Calm down,' he said, handing Ruby a glass of water.

But she pushed aside the glass, and said angrily, 'I did as I was told. You cannot throw me into the water now.'

'We can do as we like,' Anton shouted back angrily.

'Both of you, shut up!' yelled Jayesh, losing his temper. 'You are not in a fish market.'

Decorum was immediately restored in the room.

'What happened?' asked Jayesh, softening his tone, and gesturing to Anton to speak out.

'Balwant wants to take her to the hotel. If we deny his request, he won't dance. More than two million dollars are riding on him, and another three million on his troupe.'

'Hmm!'

Jayesh wondered what to do next. He took a long puff of his cigar, staring at the ceiling, making sure that he didn't make eye contact with Ruby. He was sympathetic towards her. But, losing a smaller battle for larger victory was the need of the hour. She would have to deal with this one on her own.

'Two million dollars! What the fuck!,' he said finally, after what must have been a full minute, still staring at the ceiling. He wanted to bolster Anton to the point of overconfidence. He didn't have to glance at him to see the wide smile on his face. Anton was so predictable.

Ruby stared at him shocked, and hope gave way to despair in her heart. She had expected Jayesh to stand by her, but obviously something had changed. He reminded her of an old lion who was well past his prime, with broken teeth and worn-out claws, waiting anxiously for the day when it would all be over. She stood up and stared at him, and he looked away. She thought she could see the helplessness in his eyes.

Despondently, she left the room, followed by Anton.

DEBTS MUST BE PAID

Anton returned home well past midnight, happily whistling a tune from his favourite movie. He felt that he had settled all scores with Ruby. It was a sweet victory.

Life seemed to be looking up. With improvement in cash flows expected, it was only a matter of time before Bobby won the crown. And Bobby had promised that Jack would report to him. This was something he had desired for a long time. The thought of breaking Jack down made him smile gleefully.

He stepped into the house, locking the door behind him, reached out to switch on the lights, and froze. There was the distinct outline of a person sitting by the window. Before he could react in any way, a calm voice that sent a shiver down his spine said, 'sit down, Anton.'

He didn't need to see who it was; he recognised the voice. Jesse, the head of the drug mafia, was in his house and that wasn't good news.

As his eyes adjusted to the darkness in the room, his mind raced, wondering whether to make a dash for the pistol kept in the cupboard, or run out of the house.

But before he could come to any decision, the man spoke again, 'Don't do anything stupid. We would have killed you by now had we wanted.'

Anton reluctantly walked towards the sofa in the living room and sat down.

'Pour him a drink,' said the voice.

The lights were turned on and Anton was handed a drink. He saw the faces of the people in the house and thanked his lucky stars that he hadn't done anything stupid. There were the regular suspects, the twins, Fatso and Baldy. And there was this third guy he didn't know.

'I wasn't expecting you, Jesse,' said Anton. 'Otherwise, I would have come home earlier.'

'I very much doubt it, my friend. We have been trying to reach you for some time now.'

'I have been caught up in work. We are opening a new casino.'

'All that is fine, but you are overdue.'

'I am late by a few weeks, so what? You know I will pay up.'

'We run a business, Anton, much like yourself. Such delays send wrong signals in the market. Pay up, and we'll be on our way out.'

Anton knew he was in trouble. He didn't have the money to pay. He tried to wriggle out of the situation. 'I always pay up, Jesse, you know that. I am due for a promotion. Your money is safe with me.'

Jesse didn't say a word.

'Come on man, for old times' sake,' Anton begged, Jesse's silence frightening him.

Suddenly, Fatso and the unknown man lunged towards him and pinned him down to the floor. Baldy slipped a plastic bag over his head, holding it tightly round his neck. Jesse looked on calmly, sipping his whiskey. Anton began to suffocate, gasping for air, his legs kicking frantically against the centre table of the living room. As he choked, his face turned deep red and the kicking less frantic.

Jesse gestured for the bag to be removed, 'He's no good to me dead.'

Anton struggled back to life, coughing and gasping for air. Jesse waited for a few seconds, then asked him again to pay up. When Anton didn't reply, he gestured for process to be repeated.

'You fat bastard,' he said. 'We will do this the whole night till you break. You seem to have forgotten who the boss is.'

Once again Anton was choked to within inches of his life. This time when the bag was removed, Anton looked up at Jesse and tried to speak, but his throat hurt from the choking and no voice came out.

'Give him some water,' Jesse told his men. 'The son of bitch is trying to say something.'

Anton drank the water and after a minute or two, he said, 'I don't have the money to pay up. But I have a plan which will make you rich.'

'Go on,' said Jesse, leaning forward.

When Anton had finished speaking, Jesse mulled over what he had said for a few minutes, calmly sipping his whiskey.

'If you double-cross us, we will kill you,' he said.

'Am I crazy that I would double-cross you?' replied Anton. 'I wouldn't dare.'

Jesse nodded and stood up to leave. But before Anton could heave a sigh of relief, he said, 'You still haven't paid, Anton. A price has to be paid.'

Anton shrieked in horror as three men again pinned him down to the floor. Jesse walked up to him calmly, and took the pliers that Baldy held out. He held Anton's left foot down with one hand and pulled out his toe nail with a single jerk. Anton screamed.

'I collect these,' he said with a smile.

A few minutes later they walked out of the house, leaving Anton sobbing in pain on the floor, a pool of blood round his foot. They didn't notice the red vehicle parked at some distance from the house. The private detective took photos of the men as they walked out of Anton's house. He could hear Anton wailing in the background.

The next day, the photographs were delivered to Jayesh in a sealed envelope. Jayesh went through them with amusement. He wondered how Anton had managed to wriggle out of this mess. He put the envelope safely in his locker. It would be used at an opportune moment.

ALL SHE WANTED WAS LOVE

Ruby tossed and turned in bed, wondering how she had arrived at such a point in her life. There was no place for emotions in her line of work. That was the rule from time immemorial. How could she allow herself to fall in love with a customer? But love has a way of creeping in unawares and she had little say in the matter. She was only human after all.

It had started almost two and half years ago. She had been working at the casino for only a few months. Her vibrant personality and beauty were already attracting people and she was very popular. Patrons at the casino tried to outbid each other to have her sit by their side as they gambled. They all wanted her, but she was not on the menu, adding to the mystique surrounding her.

One day, Jayesh made a startling discovery as he examined the revenue records of the casino. He found an uncanny correlation between the losses incurred by a gambler and his successful bid for Ruby. The statistics were almost surreal. Any player who had bid for Ruby almost always lost money that night. Jayesh called Ruby a 'Cooler', a person who could stop dead any high-roller in the midst of his winning streak. This quality made her a big asset for the casino and was exploited to the hilt by both Jayesh and Anton. In the beginning, Ruby also enjoyed the power she wielded and the attention she garnered from the management, especially having direct access to Jayesh, the owner of the casino. Even Anton, who had made no bones about his dislike for her, accepted that she was a great asset.

But good times seldom last for long, as Ruby soon discovered. The gambling community was close-knit and superstitious. It didn't take them long to figure out what Jayesh and Anton had known for a while, that their luck took a turn for the worse on the arrival of 'Miss Beautiful'. Within a few months, word had spread throughout the community that Miss Ruby was to be avoided at all costs. From being an object of desire fought over by the high-rollers, Ruby suddenly found herself relegated to the status of an untouchable. While some simply refused to entertain her, others were more vocal, directing their anger and frustration towards her. One night, a sophisticated, suit-wearing, high-roller, who had had a few whiskies too many, vent his frustration on her, abusing her for his loss and spitting on her face. The joke that went about in the gambling circles was that the probability of the sun not rising in the morning was higher than the probability of winning with Ruby sitting by your side.

But however hostile the environment became; Ruby got no respite from Anton. He relished every moment of her discomfort, making sure that she was in the middle of the ring every evening with her million-dollar smile. But doing her job was difficult. The old high-rollers didn't want anything to do with her and the newcomers caught on pretty fast.

It was in the midst of this that she ran into Balwant for the first time. He had seen the drunk gambler abuse her, and had walked up to her and asked, 'You all right? He is very drunk, you know.' She didn't know who he was, except for what she had heard from the other girls. On the outside, he was supposed to be uncouth and rustic with a weird sense of dressing. But the girls were unanimous that he was kind-hearted and generous. Ruby was touched by his concern and accepted him with open arms over the suit wearing gentleman who spoke with an Oxford accent but spat on her face. And thus began an unlikely liaison between the two of them. She needed him to keep Anton off her back. So long as she was with him, she was doing her job and could not be questioned. But why Balwant needed her, she didn't quite understand.

As expected, within days of meeting Balwant, her streak of bad luck had rubbed off on him, and he started to lose regularly. In the beginning, she didn't feel any remorse for him. On the contrary, she used her position of strength to take potshots at Anton, who was keeping a close eye on her. Anton knew that it was only a matter of time before Balwant figured out what the other high-rollers had realised before him and threw her off. But, as weeks passed, Anton began to suspect Balwant's intelligence. He was disappointed, for he would have liked nothing more than to see Ruby get completely rejected. On one hand, he knew that Ruby was very useful for the casino, on the other, he disliked her for who she was and enjoyed her humiliation

'You lucky bitch,' he once told her, 'you have found yourself a drunk dimwit.'

The weeks became months and months became a year and Ruby began to feel bad about Balwant's losses. Here was a guy who lost money consistently for over a year and still wanted her beside him. He was at the casino twice or thrice a fortnight, losing money on every occasion. But, no matter the quantum of his loss, he was always kind and considerate to her.

After feeling guilty for a few weeks, Ruby decided to confront him. She downed a few whiskies and pulled him to the deck for a quiet conversation.

'Why are you so nice to me?' she asked. 'Don't you see I bring bad luck?'

Balwant smiled and replied, 'I feel for you. We are both alike.'

'How is that?' she asked.

'We are both outcasts. I protect you from them.'

'But, don't you see that you lose money because of me,' she argued.

He smiled again, 'There is no such thing as bad luck. Don't blame yourself for my loss.'

Ruby cried that night. If she had felt guilty earlier, she felt even worse now. For the first time, someone had treated her like a human being and not as an object of desire or hate. She had experienced selfless affection. Balwant had protected her from the hounds at the casino at the cost of losing money. It was bizarre. She wanted to believe that she was being superstitious, that there was no such thing as bad luck, and that she was not responsible for him losing. But, no matter how hard she tried, she felt guilty. The results stared back at her in black and white.

As months passed, her fondness for him increased and so did her guilt. Despite his large and slightly uncouth appearance, he was warm and gentle. She began to despise herself for what she did to him. For the first time in her life, she cared for someone else. She tried more than once to tell him to stay away from her, but he absolutely refused.

Finally, she decided to tell him the truth about herself. She was no beautiful woman—she was a ladyboy. Perhaps, this would succeed where all else had failed. But, when the time came to walk the talk, her knees turned to jelly. She couldn't do it. At that moment, she realised how much he meant to her. All her life she had craved love and affection. She remembered her first sexual encounter when she was only 14 years old. The man had pretended to be loving and gentle. But what transpired had left her feeling empty and disappointed. It had happened again and again. Men pursued her for sexual release whereas she was seeking something more emotional and permanent, a companionship. Who was she kidding? There was no way that she was going to reveal the truth to him. Not yet. She was human, and like all humans she was selfish. She couldn't bear to lose him. What if he walked away from her life, her only source of hope and light in a mundane life bereft of love.

Ever since that day, she has lived in conflict, hating herself for not being truthful. But the alternative was unimaginable. For, no one had ever showered affection on her like Balwant had for the past two years. And now, when she deeply desired him, and could no longer live without him, the truth would finally be revealed. She wondered what the outcome would be. Would he walk out on her, feeling cheated that she had hidden her true identity from him all this time? Would he give her an opportunity to say something in her defence? And, what defence could she put up for herself? That she was selfish and in love with him? Whatever the outcome, she would have to accept it, for life was cruel indeed.

PART 2

THE BIGGEST GAME OF HIS LIFE

Mr and Mrs Chaddha sat near the gate, waiting for the boarding announcement to be made. They were well known Delhi socialites on their way to their holiday home in Goa. The Delhi–Goa flight sector is amongst the busiest in India, with 14 direct flights on weekdays and 17 on weekends, and the boarding lounge was teeming with people of all colours and sizes, displaying the regional and cultural diversity of India.

'Look at them,' said Mrs Chaddha with disdain, staring at a group of people. 'Loud and uncouth *dehatis* (folk from rural India).'

Her own voice was not discreet. It reflected her sense of entitlement simply because she belonged to a certain social class which she believed was superior. Her statement, on this occasion, was directed towards a group of villagers, dressed in simple collared shirts and trousers—not necessarily of the best fit, nor colour coordinated—chewing tobacco and loud in their chatter. They all belonged to the same village, but Balwant wasn't amongst them. He was still comfortably ensconced in the lounge, waiting for boarding to be announced.

Mr Chaddha lowered the morning paper covering his face and looked up. He smiled and assured her, 'Don't worry darling! A few more minutes and we will be away from this hullabaloo.'

They were travelling business class.

'I hope you have taken two aisle seats?' she asked.

'Of course, darling, as always.'

Reassured, she went back to reading her magazine about the latest trends in the world of fashion.

As soon as boarding for the flight was announced, a relieved Mr & Mrs Chaddha rushed to occupy their seats, followed by the masses.

Balwant continued to sit in the lounge picking his nose. It was only when he heard his name being announced on the P.A system that he finally stood up and began to walk towards the boarding gate. He always made it a point to be the last person to board a flight. Important people always boarded at the very end, keeping others waiting. After all, if you didn't value your own time, then why would anyone else value you?

He was dressed casually today, in a pair of Armani Jeans, bally shoes and a Fred Perry Polo; his beard was neatly trimmed and his hair was cut in the latest style, just like his fashion idol —Virat Kohli.

The airhostess recognised him and greeted him with a warm smile which he reciprocated. But, Mrs Chaddha, who had by this time made herself quite comfortable in her aisle seat, gave him a cold look.

'Excuse me, madam,' he said, in an accent reflecting his education at a Hindi medium school.

She did not move an inch, her legs stretched out, blocking the way to the window seat. 'He must have the wrong seat number,' she said disdainfully to no one in particular.

Once Balwant would have felt uncomfortable at the cold, condescending look and would have hidden himself behind a magazine or pretended to look elsewhere. But that was long ago when he was still trying hard to blend in, to be accepted in urban high society. But ever since it had dawned on him that no matter how much money he had, the divide between rural and urban India was there to stay, the warmth had given way to aggression, and the simplicity had been replaced by vanity.

'*Asli hai*, madam (It is real),' he said with a grin, when he saw her looking at the twenty-thousand-dollar Rolex on his wrist, its gold strap shining under the light. The cheeky statement had the desired effect on Mrs Chaddha who not only withdrew her outstretched legs, but also exchanged seats with her husband. Unperturbed, Balwant settled himself comfortably in his window seat.

He was looking forward to the evening. There was much at stake tonight. The largest casino in the country was being inaugurated by Jayesh Shah, the kingpin of the gambling industry in India. The who's who of the gambling world were invited. In keeping with his past reputation, he has wagered the biggest game of his life, taking on a credit of two million dollars from the casino; and he hoped to take his relationship with Ruby to the next level. Over the past two years, their affection for each other had been growing and he has, for the first time, asked her out for the night.

The air hostess announced that the plane was ready for the take-off and he put on his seat belt and closed his eyes. Despite frequent air travel, he still wasn't comfortable with take-offs and landings. Within minutes, he was fast asleep, much to the relief of Mr Chaddha.

WE HAVE YOUR SON

It was the perfect winter afternoon with the sun shining brightly and a cool breeze blowing in from the sea. The air was thick with the aroma of Goanese sausage vindaloo. Louis, dressed in Bermuda shorts and an open white shirt, a can of beer in one hand and a large wooden spoon in the other, jived to the tune of Bob Marley playing in the background, putting finishing touches to the dish. Vindaloo was Pinchoo's favourite dish. His young son meant the world to Louis and he doted on Pinchoo. Ever since his mother had passed away while giving birth to him, Louis had played the dual role of mother and father in his life.

Louis had been dealing blackjack for over 20 years. Being a blackjack dealer wasn't as flashy as it appeared. For starters, the money wasn't very good. The salary was just about enough to meet his expenses. It didn't matter whether the customer was a high society gambler or a road side hustler, they all cried when they lost, and almost always it was the fault of the dealer.

Thus, he often found himself being yelled at or sometimes, even abused, for no fault of his own. It was at such times that his experience came to the fore, as what he said next or how he behaved decided the course of events. His colleagues called him 'Iceman' because he never lost his cool even in the worst of circumstances. This had earned him the respect and admiration of the customers and management alike. On the other hand, when the tides turned, the same customers who yelled at him and abused him when they lost, became his best pals, showering him with praises and lavish tips. It was all part of the game that made it worth being a dealer.

He was looking forward to the grand inauguration of the new casino later that evening. Louis was proud that the management has selected him from amongst the many blackjack dealers to deal at this important event. He was hoping to cash in on some of his popularity in the evening, expecting some gracious tips from his high-roller clients.

He took one last whiff of the vindaloo before turning off the gas and garnishing it with coriander. Then he glanced at the old grandfather clock hanging on the wall. It was time to lay the table. Pinchoo would be arriving any moment now. He laid the table, then cleaned the kitchen. Pinchoo still hadn't come. He started clearing up the drawing room, looking out of the window every few minutes. When there was still no sign of Pinchoo, he began to get restless. While he was a model of self-composure at work, Louis had a heart of butter when it came to Pinchoo. The smallest of things got him anxious. He cursed himself for not having given his son a mobile phone, an item of luxury not long ago, and now a necessity. Finally, after waiting for fifteen minutes, he put on his hat, and walked towards the bus stop. It was only a five-minute walk, but with every successive step, his heart beat louder. He hoped that nothing untoward had happened to Pinchoo.

Where could Pinchoo be? Had he forgotten to tell him about an afterschool event? That was likely and here he was worrying that the world was ending. His mind was still not at ease, but he put on a brave smile and decided to walk back home and eat the meal he had prepared. He would leave a large part for Pinchoo who would surely come home tired and hungry.

He had only taken a few steps when he received a call on his phone from an unknown number. His heart hammered and he immediately answered.

'Pinchoo?' he said aloud.

There was no response except for the sound of deep breathing on the other side.

'Pinchoo? Is that you?' he repeated, more anxiously.

This time a muffled voice replied, 'Pinchoo is in our custody. He is eating a sandwich and drinking soda as we speak.'

'Who is this?' Louis cried aloud.

'That is not relevant,' replied the muffled voice. 'But what I say next, is. So, listen very carefully. Pinchoo will not be harmed as long as you do as I say.'

Harmed? Had he heard that correctly? This was surreal, a bad dream. What could anyone want from him? He was a poor, honest soul trying to make a living. Fear gripped his heart and his legs gave in. He collapsed onto the footpath.

'Are you still there?' said the muffled voice.

'Yes,' he replied, recovering from the initial shock. 'There's been some mistake. I am a poor man. What could you want from me?'

'There's been no mistake. Aren't you Louis, the senior blackjack dealer at the Renaissance Casino?'

It began to make sense to him. They weren't after him at all, it was his employer they wanted.

'Please let my son go,' he said. 'He has nothing to do with this.'

'Meet us at 12:00 am at the toilet on the second floor of the casino. Make sure you are alone.'

'At least allow me to speak to Pinchoo once?' he cried.

'Listen, dickhead, you are in no position to negotiate,' said the muffled voice, now sounding infuriated. 'Do as we say, otherwise you will be responsible for what happens to your Pinchoo.'

'No! No! Don't do anything to him,' he begged. 'I will do as you ask. But there is electronic surveillance at the casino.'

'Don't worry about the surveillance. It has been taken care of.'

'I will be there. Don't harm my son.'

'Do as we say and you have nothing to worry about. Your son will be sleeping in his bed before you return from work. But, should you decide to act adventurous, he will be sleeping with the fish at the bottom of the river.'

The call was disconnected.

THERE ARE NO SIMPLE MISUNDERSTANDINGS

Jack parked his car by the jetty. A speed boat was waiting to take him to MV Sultan which was anchored in the middle of the Mandovi river. In a few hours, the ship would be transformed into the largest live gaming casino in the country. For the past fortnight, he has spent more time on the ship than in his house, testing the robustness of the surveillance systems.

As the speed boat made its way towards the ship, he looked back at the city of Panaji with affection. The city has been home to him for the past several years. This was the city where he had met the love of his life and with whom he was now planning to start a new adventure, a new life. He had a job offer now at a casino in Singapore which he has accepted. Tonight, after this grand inauguration, he planned to put in his papers.

A few weeks earlier, he had found himself in the midst of a dilemma, being pulled in two opposite directions. At one end was his conscience, which told him that he couldn't absolve himself of the responsibility of the wrongdoings at the casino merely by closing his eyes and looking elsewhere. He couldn't feign ignorance and was complicit in the money laundering that was being carried out. The only way out of this predicament was to quit his job. But he felt guilty about walking out on Jayesh, the man who had stood behind him like a rock through the good and bad times in Goa. After many sleepless nights, he approached Jayesh for advice. It was only after Jayesh himself encouraged him to look for a new job that he was finally able to resolve his issues and get a good night of sleep.

His new employer had also offered Nisha a job. In fact, they were even more excited about meeting her than him. It was rare to meet a person who was worthy of the Griffins list (cheats, frauds and players with superior skills who are unwelcome in a casino because of their high rate of winning), but not actually on it. The possibilities were infinite. They wanted her to play a mystery customer at the casino to see how robust their systems were. Nisha was a bit rustic, but Jack was sure that she would be in her elements in no time. All they needed to do was give her a challenge and then let her loose. He was confident that she would give them a run for their money.

Back home, his father was still playing the tough guy. As the head of the family, he downplayed his emotions and pretended indifference. Emotions were for the weak. Real men didn't cry. But Jack knew that it was all playacting and he was delighted that his son was coming home. Remove the top layer and his father was all jelly. He hoped to convince his old man to take life easy and pass on the responsibility of the family to him.

Jack arrived at the casino and greeted everyone on his team. They had all worked hard to create the online surveillance system. Tonight was the night of reckoning when it would all come together. It was one thing to test the system in a controlled environment and quite another to see it running live. He hoped that there were no surprises and that everything went as per plan. He would have preferred to try out the system at a soft launch with a few customers, but Jayesh had refused to do any soft launches. He didn't want the surprise element to be lost. News always leaked in the social media. He wanted to awe his guests as they walked into the grand casino. As a result, here they were, launching the largest casino in the country on the back of a surveillance system which had never gone live before.

Jack sat down at his desk. He was a little tense, which was generally a good sign and meant that he was well prepared. He picked up the sealed envelope lying on his desk and ripped it open. Inside, on a sheet of paper, were a few numbers without any corresponding explanation. To an outsider they would have made no sense. But Jack knew exactly what they stood for and what was required of him. The numbers highlighted the cameras which were to be switched off.

As he went down the list, he came across an anomaly. He and Anton had reached an implicit understanding that no more than three cameras would be switched off in any of the casinos on a given night. But, in the list that he now held in his hand, Anton had asked for four cameras in the newest casino to be switched off on the opening night.

Jack mulled over the request. Should he raise it as an issue or let it pass? Could it be a simple case of misunderstanding? In the past, all their discussions had revolved around the older casinos. They had never discussed the operations of the new casino. This casino was much bigger in size than any of the others. It could be a simple case of logical deduction. *Anton could have deduced that if I was comfortable with switching off three cameras in the smaller casinos, I would not object when he suggested four for the larger one.*

He wondered if he should run the request by Jayesh. Then he remembered Jayesh telling him, 'Give Anton some slack. I know where he is coming from.' *I shouldn't bother him. He already has too much on his platter and doesn't need me to add to his troubles.*

Perhaps, the best thing to do was to make a quick call to Anton. Tell him that he had received his request. It was an exception, but he had decided to play along in camaraderie. *I have to be very careful with my words. I don't want Anton to feel that I am putting him on the spot.* He dialled Anton on the intercom. The bell rang a few times but there was no response. *Must be on the floor.*

Should he call him on his mobile? No point, it would never connect.

How juvenile of me! I will be resigning tomorrow morning and here I am still trying to cover my ass and show one-upmanship. Why should I care about any of this? He stood up from his seat and walked out of his room towards the refrigerator, got a can of cola and went to his surveillance team. He instructed them to switch off the relevant cameras. Then he walked back into his room and put the envelope along with its contents into the shredder. He didn't want any of this hanky-panky to be traced back to him. One more day of this shit and then it will be all over. This was the reason he wanted out.'

Meanwhile, Anton was at his desk in the lower deck of the ship. He saw the extension number as the intercom rang. He smiled. *The son of a bitch must have seen the envelope. He must be twisting in his chair.*

He had no intention of answering the call. Everything was carefully orchestrated to make Jack think there might be a simple misunderstanding. Jack didn't know it but he had walked into a trap. Anton was going to give him one hell of a parting gift.

AND THE PARTY BEGINS

A live band was playing popular Bollywood numbers at the jetty, where nearly twenty motor boats waited to ferry guests to the MV Sultan. Karishma and her photographer paused to look at the beautifully decorated motor boats and the boatmen dressed in sailor suits with the logo of the MV Sultan. She was amused to see that there were even some gondolas making a more leisurely way to the ship. Crowds had gathered to see the spectacle and spot celebrities going to the casino. It was a little after eight in the evening. Guests had already begun to arrive and were being escorted with great fanfare to the motorboats and off to the ship. Karishma turned from the band and the boats to look farther into the sea where the MV Sultan was docked. The ship sat like a glittering jewel on the black ocean. It was lit up with thousands of lights and every few minutes fireworks lit up the evening sky.

Karishma flashed her VIP invite to the concierge and was immediately whisked past the crowds to a lounge where glasses of champagne and finger food awaited them. Karishma pecked at a hors d'oeuvre, while Gopal, her photographer, filled a small plate and accepted some bubbly. The concierge reappeared offering them a choice of transport: a private motor launch or a romantic Gondola. Before Gopal could say a word, Karishma asked for thc motor boat. She just wanted to get to the casino as soon as possible. 'We must remember we are here on work,' she said to him.

A few minutes later they arrived at the MV Sultan where an attractively dressed hostess immediately took charge of them and showed them round the ship. At the end of the tour, they were handed goody bags which contained playing chips. Karishma asked to see Jayesh Shah and was told that he would soon be there to meet all his guests.

'Until he comes, let's try our luck with these chips, shall we?' said Gopal and they walked to the slot machines.

Ruby rushed into Jayesh's chamber just as he was leaving for the casino where guests had already started arriving. She had received a call from Bobby asking her to provide two specific girls for a VIP customer later that night. There was nothing unusual about the request. Many customers wanted to have two girls. But this customer was different. He took the definition of kinky sex to another level altogether. On a previous occasion, the girls had returned psychologically traumatised and didn't want to go back to him.

'Where were you?' Jayesh asked, as he slipped into his jacket. 'People have started arriving.'

'I was on a call with Bobby. I need to discuss something with you,' she replied.

'Can this wait? We are already running late. And I have to be there to meet someone.'

He saw her agitated expression and said, 'Ok! Be quick. What is it?'

'Firstly, you wanted me to escort Balwant. As if that wasn't bad enough…'

'I have no time for Balwant,' interrupted Jayesh. 'Get to the point. Tell me there is something else?'

'Bobby has asked me to send two of the youngest girls to a customer later tonight. I don't know who this VIP customer is, but he has been here before and he is one hell of a kinky bastard.'

'So? What is wrong with that?'

'The girls are scared of him. They don't want to go.'

'Excuse me? You don't get to choose your clients!' said Jayesh, losing his patience. 'You run an escort service. You are a *Mamasan*, not their mother. You make sure that they attend to the customer.'

'But this one is sick in the head. He colours them in gold and forces them to perform unspeakable acts.'

There was a sudden change in Jayesh's expression. There was only one person he knew who did the 'Goldfinger Act'. Was this person visiting the casino without informing him?

That too on the night of the grand inauguration! Publicly, he would not been seen anywhere near it, so he was going to creep in. Indeed, this might be a blessing in disguise. Jayesh's shrewd mind started churning. Since he was not in the know, he could always feign ignorance for any mishaps that may happen later that evening.

'Boss, do you know this VIP customer?' Ruby asked, interrupting his racing thoughts.

'No. I don't know who it is,' he said. But she guessed from his expression that he had some idea of who this man could be.

'Aren't you going to do anything about it?'

'Has this client physically hurt any of the girls?'

'No, but he has psychologically scarred them for life.'

'Ruby, you are stretching this argument too far. Unless you feel that the girls are in physical danger, we can't do anything. We can't police what the client thinks in his mind. I tell you what, I will compensate the girls well for their trouble. That's the best I can do.'

Ruby knew that it was pointless to argue any further.

'Shall we now go to the casino floor?'

'Of course,' she said, walking besides him, holding his arm.

'Who are you supposed to meet?' she asked.

'A young journalist called Karishma. She is one hell of a time bomb. Always looking out for a scoop. Maybe her desires will be fulfilled tonight.'

THEY ARE ALL FAKE

Jayesh and Ruby entered the casino to flashing cameras and the regular greet and meet. After the first few minutes of excitement had died down, Ruby asked him if she should move away.

'Not yet. Let's schmooze around for a while.'

'But I thought you were late for an appointment?'

'Yes, I was' he replied. "But that was before you told me about the Goldfinger Act. There is someone I must introduce you to before I move on.'

Before Ruby could ask him anything more, Jayesh turned to his right and exclaimed, 'Look who we have here! Hello, Jill,' he gave the attractive lady an affectionate peck on the cheek. 'I am delighted to see you.'

'Thank you for inviting me,' she replied.

'Please don't say that,' he said, looking a bit embarrassed. 'We never forget our own.'

'Some have forgotten,' she replied, curtly.

Jayesh ignored that and said, ‘Have you two girls met?’

‘Of course, we have,’ replied Ruby. ‘How are you darling?’ she said, giving Jill a big hug.

‘I am the same old,’ replied Jill. ‘Only a little older since we met last. How about you?’

‘I must confess, I have been better,’ said Ruby, not bothering to mince her words.

‘Not again,’ said Jayesh raising his hands in the air.

‘Why? What happened?’ asked Jill.

Before Ruby could speak a word, Jayesh cut in.

‘Girls, why don’t I leave you two to gossip.’

‘Why such a hurry?’ asked Jill.

‘Darling, she has already ranted her frustrations before me. Besides, I have a prior appointment.’

‘Where is this imaginary journalist that you are supposed to meet?’ asked Ruby, cheekily. ‘I hope you are not making an excuse to get away from us.’

‘Why would I move away from two beautiful women?’ replied Jayesh. ‘See, my imaginary friend, that young girl in the corner, the one with the photographer?’

Karishma was busy chatting with the page 3 glitterati in the lounge while Gopal busied himself taking pictures.

'That's a sexy evening gown, Ma'am,' she said to the smartly dressed old lady.

'Oh, it's a Versace. I bought it from Milan only last fortnight.'

'Ooh! I love that neck line.'

'Ha-ha! I say flaunt it so long as you have it.'

'Those are fake darling,' said a voice coming from another lady standing behind her. 'This is the real stuff.'

'And you are?' asked Karishma.

'It doesn't matter,' retorted the first woman. 'We call her Miss K-Pop. Look at her nose, cheeks, lips. She has been through a complete overhaul.'

Before the two ladies could get into a no-holds-barred squabbling match, Karishma intervened, gesturing to Gopal to take a few shots. Almost immediately any angst they had against each other disappeared and they merrily hugged and kissed for the photographs. It was clear that they had done this before, posing to highlight the best their bodies had to offer.

They even asked Gopal all details of the newspaper.

'When will it be published?'

'I hope it is a colour edition?'

'Make sure you get my name right,' said the first one. 'It is Sheila Parik. That is Parik ending with a K and not an H'.

Karishma walked away looking for something or someone more interesting. A minute later, she yelled, 'Oh My God!' as she moved towards Kumar Saurabh with her arms spread wide open for a hug. Kumar Saurabh didn't know who she was, but was delighted by her reaction. He immediately obliged her with a hug.

'Sir, my mother is such a fan! Could I have a photograph with you?' she requested.

'Of course. My pleasure,' replied Kumar Saurabh suavely, as if such attention came to him all the time and was his due.

Gopal took a few snaps in different configurations. As they moved away, he asked Karishma, 'Who is he?'

'A fading star,' she replied.

'You mean a Bollywood star? How come I didn't recognise him?'

'Darling, that is because his last big hit was before either of us were born.'

'How do you know him?' he asked.

'I didn't know of his existence till last week,' she confessed. 'I read up on him after Jayesh told me that he was going to be here today.'

'And your mother? Is she a fan?'

'No, *baba*. That was all an act.'

'Wow. Karishma, you should be at the National School of Drama. What are you doing as a journalist?'

'I do what is required to get my story. At this moment, I am getting bored.'

'Why?'

'There is no variety here. They are all fake.'

'What do you mean?'

'You know, they are all so made up, attention starved, with fake smiles, fake boobs, Botox ruling the roost.'

'What else did you expect at a page three event?'

'I don't know. Perhaps, I expected too much. But a part of me wanted to see something new, something different, a new trend. They are all identical, so similar, they look the same, they suffer from the same insecurities, they are influenced by the same triggers.'

'Don't sound so bored. Let me find something interesting for you. How about that Kohli lookalike?'

'Where?' she asked excitedly.

The photographer gestured with his eyes.

'No,' she said, disappointedly. 'He looks nothing like my favourite player.'

'Maybe, he doesn't. But, that's variety,' he replied.

'Hmm! On second thoughts, it is worth exploring. There is something about him that's different in this setting.'

THERE IS ALWAYS HOPE

'For the first time in my life, I have found a person who treats me like a human being and not some object of desire,' said Ruby. 'I feel like a woman in his company.'

'I totally understand what you are saying, darling,' said Jill. 'There was a time in my life when I felt the same way. But this story never has a happy ending. You cannot fall in love in your line of work.'

'I know, I understand what you are saying,' replied Ruby. 'But I am helpless. My heart yearns for him.'

'Oh lord! You must be miserable.'

'Imagine! A man who has only given me love, and all I have given him in return is bad luck.'

'I am so sorry for you.'

'As if that wasn't bad enough, I got a call today to entertain some kinky VIP customer.'

'Oh my! You seem to be having a bad time.'

'Yeah! The son of a bitch only wants young girls.'

'Don't they always?' said Jill. 'The older they get, the younger they want.'

'This one's unique. He wants two at a time, and it doesn't stop there.'

'What do you mean?' asked Jill, curiously. 'Tell me more.'

'He has a fetish for gold colour. He first covers them in gold paint and then ties them up, gagging their mouth.'

Jill's face went tight. 'How interesting,' she said, her palms tightening around the glass of wine she was holding.

'Then he engages in rough sex with one of them, while forcing the other to watch.'

The stem of the wine glass broke in Jill's hand as many Friday evenings from several years earlier flashed before her eyes.

'Oh, what happened? Are you alright?' exclaimed Ruby, quickly calling a passing waiter to pick up the broken glass and examining Jill's fingers to see if there was a cut.

'Yeah! I am fine,' said Jill, displaying her fingers front and back. 'Your story is both dark and engaging at the same time.'

'I am so sorry. I have been so insensitive. It's just that it's been playing on my mind.'

'No, no. Please tell me more. I am curious about what he does with the other girl.'

'Nothing. He lets her go. But, as she is about to leave, he whispers in her ears that he is saving her for the next time.

'How interesting. He instils fear in them. The poor girls must be traumatised.'

'Oh yes! They don't want to go back to him. But they don't have a choice.

'Hmm! So where is this crazy story playing out tonight?'

'Where else? The Presidential Suite. That's where all the crazy stuff happens.'

'Don't you have to send them now?'

'No! The VIP arrives at 1:00 am, away from the eyes of the general public.'

'The girls better start drinking now. Give them a few shots of tequila before they go to him. It will help to calm their nerves.'

'Wow! A farmer turned gambler,' said Karishma. 'How interesting!'

'Madam, what makes it interesting?' asked Balwant.

'Please don't get me wrong, but I didn't expect a farmer in this gathering.'

Balwant smiled. The same stereotype of rural India, even with the so-called educated journalists.

'Madam, I beg to differ. You couldn't be more wrong. I can bet with you that if you were to do a survey on the casino floor, you will find that the largest number of people represent the farming community.'

'What? Are you serious?' said Karishma, surprised.

'Yes. Also, unlike those ladies who were posing for photographs, we come here to play.'

'I see. May I ask, why are so many farmers attracted to gambling?'

'India is evolving and so are its villages. There are many affluent people living in rural areas with cash to spare. They don't have the exposure, but they have aspirations just like their counterparts in the city. They need a source of entertainment like anyone else.'

'So, according to you, it is the entertainment that attracts them to the casinos?'

'Initially, it is the entertainment. Who doesn't like free-flowing alcohol and women? But then they get hooked on to gambling.'

'But, shouldn't free-flowing alcohol and women appear equally appealing to city folks?'

'That's where exposure comes into play. Village folk are gullible and more vulnerable to the marketing activities of the casinos.'

'Forgive me, Balwant, but you don't look very gullible, you know.'

'Ha-ha! There was a time when I used to be. I lost a lot of money before I lost my naivety. It was an expensive learning.'

'Now I am curious. What gets a guy like Balwant to the casino? Do you win quite often?'

'No. On the contrary, I lose a lot.'

'Why do you come here? You come across as a logical, intelligent person. Why come when you know that you are going to lose?'

'Because there is always hope. Human beings have a positive bias. We see light when there is none. We wake up every morning with the hope that things will become better. Then, I have my own personal reasons.'

'Like what? Can you tell me? I am intrigued.'

'The casino is a refuge for me. I am accepted here with open arms, no longer an outcast. I find this very liberating. They don't judge me on the basis of my background, caste or creed. The only thing that matters to them is the money in my pocket, and so long as I have plenty to spare, I am always welcome.'

'But you do know that their affection is fake. They love your money. They welcome only as long as you have plenty to spare.'

'Ha-ha! Karishma, I wonder in which world you live? Are you suggesting that the world outside is not fake? That people don't love you for your money. At least, in here I know what I am getting into.'

'I apologise if I have offended you.'

'Not at all. I am too thick-skinned to get offended.'

'This is by far the most interesting discussion I have had this evening,' she said.

'Ha-ha! You weren't expecting that, were you? These days, almost all philosophy originates in the villages.'

'Why is that?'

'They are the only ones who have time to think. All they do is smoke hookahs and talk. City folk are so busy trying to make a living that they seldom have time to do much else.'

'Wow! You have completely changed my perspective. I must make a trip to the hinterland.'

'And this one is just warming up,' said Jayesh, joining the conversation.

'Oh yes! Balwant has been enlightening me about rural India. I must confess, I know very little.'

'Balwant, you never cease to surprise me,' said Jayesh. 'I believe you are playing a big hand tonight. I came to wish you good luck.'

'Thanks, Jayesh. You are a good sport. Let me warn you that I am feeling lucky tonight. With Ruby by my side, nothing can go wrong.'

'Who is Ruby?' asked Karishma.

'She is my lucky charm.'

'Oh! Is she? I would love to meet her.'

Ruby was curiously watching the interaction between Balwant and Karishma from a distance. She was surprised that the conversation had gone on for so long. Balwant was a man of few words. She wondered what they were discussing.

When Jayesh also decided to join the group, Ruby could no longer hold herself back.

'Come on, darling,' she told Jill. 'Let me introduce you to the love of my life.'

'Where is he?' Jill asked.

'Over there. Look at that guy standing with Jayesh.'

'Isn't that the journalist?' she asked.

'Oh yes! The journalist is also there.'

'Let us go.'

'Talk of the devil and here she is,' said Jayesh, as Ruby and Jill joined the group. 'Let me have the honour of introducing you all.'

'Karishma, this is Ruby, the head of our client relations. And, this is Jill, an old friend of mine. There is no gossip in Goa that she doesn't know.'

'Wow! Jill, you are exactly the person I want to meet. We must chat when you have time.'

'Sure,' replied Jill, a little embarrassed. 'But, don't believe everything that Jayesh tells you.'

'Come on, darling,' said Jayesh. 'Few understand the undercurrents of Goa the way you do.'

'Not the way I used to. But now that you have put me on stage, I will try to live up to your standards.'

'By the way, Ruby, we were just speaking about you,' said Karishma.

'Good things, I hope.'

'Oh yes! Balwant here has only praise for you. He calls you his lucky charm.'

'Is that so?' said Ruby, forcing a smile. 'Balwant's eyes see what no one else does.'

'That is because I have the eyes of a jeweller,' said Balwant, cheekily. 'Where others see glass, I see a diamond.'

'What if it is just glass, as everyone else suspects?' asked Jill.

'That is part and parcel of life,' replied Balwant. 'You win some, you lose some.'

THE DOMINANT DIAMOND

'I had a dream last night,' said Balwant.

'About me?' asked Ruby, coyly.

'Darling, it's almost always about you,' replied Balwant. 'But last night it was about roulette.'

'Not craps?' asked Ruby. 'After all, craps is where your heart lies.'

'No. We are going to start this evening by playing roulette.'

Balwant and Ruby made their way around the casino floor walking from one roulette table to another.

'What are you looking for?' she asked.

'I have a specific table number in mind.'

'Since when did you start believing in numerology?'

'Not numerology. Let's just say that a birdie told me that I should play on this roulette table.'

'So, it wasn't a dream?'

'Darling, some things cannot be explained rationally. You believe that you bring bad luck. Is there any explanation for it?'

Ruby was quiet. She walked silently behind Balwant, holding his hand. They kept walking till they reached one end of the casino, far away from the crowds. Balwant stopped in front of an old table that had seen significant action.

'Aah! Here it is,' he said. 'Table 38. This is the table I saw in my dream.'

To Ruby, it looked like any other table. A little older, perhaps. But Balwant knew exactly why this table was special. Roulette is different from craps or blackjack where the results are random and based on probabilities. The outcomes in Roulette depend on the laws of physics. Hence, any imperfection in the wheel can give rise to non-random results.

Balwant pulled out a seat and made himself comfortable. Ruby sat next to him.

'I am going to change your pattern tonight,' he said. 'For too long, you have lived under the impression that you bring bad luck.'

The dealer, who till then had been yawning in boredom, looked at them in anticipation. He was surprised to see Balwant take a seat at his table. Balwant was a whale, one who gambled for very high stakes. Whales generally played in private rooms away from the crowds and were handled by experienced dealers. He was a novice, which is why he was manning this table located at the far end of the casino floor.

The Pit Boss, who was watching from a distance, came running. 'Sir, would you like me to change the dealer?' he asked.

'Why? What's wrong with this one?' asked Balwant.

'Nothing, sir. He is a new hand.'

'How will he ever become an old hand if you don't let him serve?' asked Balwant.

'As you wish, sir.'

Balwant asked for casino chips worth a million dollars. Then he examined the wheel of the table. He noticed the dominant diamond. One of the metal deflectors (diamonds) was more worn out than the others. To anyone with less experience of gambling, this had little relevance. But a professional gambler knew that dominant diamonds do not occur randomly. They indicate a pattern, which can be exploited to make money.

The presence of a dominant diamond implied that the ball hit a particular metal deflector more often than the others. Dominant diamonds arose due to imperfections in the wheel caused by normal wear and tear of many years of usage. Once a ball hit the dominant diamond, it would most likely fall into one of the numbered pockets below it. This was the basic premise behind the concept of visual ballistics, which have been used by professional gamblers the world over to make a killing on the Roulette table.

Balwant started by playing safe. He bet small denomination chips on high probability outcomes; like betting on colour or lines instead of numbers. The aim was not to win, but to closely observe the dealer as he spun the ball on the wheel. The ball moved on the ball track, gradually slowing down, losing momentum, and eventually falling into the wheel head. Sometimes the ball was deflected by the diamonds and fell into the numbered pockets below them. Sometimes the ball fell into the wheel base without being deflected by any of the diamonds. Then there were times when the ball bounced after hitting one of the diamonds and fell into some other sector of the wheel base rather than the one located below the diamond.

On the first spin the ball fell after 13 spins. It was 15 on the second spin. However, after a dozen spins, it became consistent at 14 spins. Balwant timed the 14 spins on his watch, which he wore on the inner side of his left wrist. He had a glass of whiskey in the same hand and sipped his drink every now and then. From the time it left the hands of the dealer to the time it fell on the wheel base; the ball took an average of 17 seconds. Now all he had to do was to figure the sector of the wheel that would be under the dominant diamond after 17 seconds. Once he had figured it out, he would bet on the entire sector i.e., five to seven numbers.

This method was not very accurate, but it didn't need to be. They were playing on a European table with a single zero number giving the casino a house advantage of only 2.7

percent. He needed only so much accuracy to beat this slight house advantage of the casino.

Balwant won a few big hands at the roulette table. It was enough to get the Pit Boss excited, but not large enough to attract too much heat. Then he abruptly stood up and left the roulette table much to Ruby's astonishment.

'Where are we going?' she asked.

'To play craps. Look at the crowd at that table,' he said.

'Why don't we continue playing roulette? We were winning.'

'I feel lucky tonight. We will win at craps too,' Balwant smiled, swallowed his whiskey and poured himself some more. Ruby gently warned him to go a little slow, but he simply smiled at her.

Soon, he had downed quite a few whiskies and began to gamble recklessly. Ruby watched helplessly as she saw him fall into the same old pattern. Why had she thought it would be any different tonight? Feeling frustrated, she decided to get herself a drink too. Maybe it would lift her spirits, or even better, change his fortune. She didn't want him to lose any more money.

NEXT TIME, IT WILL BE YOUR NECK

Ruby perched on a stool at a fair distance from Kumar Saurabh, who was sitting at the centre of the bar counter. He had been rude to her on several occasions and she was in no mood to chat with him tonight. He turned to look at her. She pretended not to see him and chatted with the bartender instead. After a few minutes, Kumar Saurabh got up and moved to a stool next to her. Now there was no way of avoiding him. She turned to face him.

'Hello, Ruby,' he said. 'You are looking a little upset tonight. All well?'

What's gotten into him? she wondered. *He is actually showing interest in my well-being?*

'It's nothing! Balwant is being himself. But thanks for asking,' said Ruby, her arms across her chest.

'I owe you an apology for my past behaviour. I have often been rude and disrespectful to you. I can't undo what has happened, but I wish to sincerely apologise.'

Ruby was surprised and taken aback. This was the last thing she had expected. 'Your apology is gladly accepted,' she said, graciously. She crossed her legs and opened her arms to sit comfortably. 'How has the evening been for you?' she asked.

'Very good,' he replied.

'Did you win some money?'

'Oh no! It's not about money. I was estranged from my only daughter,' he grimaced. 'We weren't even on talking terms. But now she has finally forgiven me. It is the best thing that could have ever happened to me!'

'Wow! That is great news indeed. Cheers to that,' she said, raising her glass.

Kumar Saurabh reciprocated the gesture.

'What does your daughter do?'

Kumar Saurabh hesitated for a few seconds, then said, 'As a matter of fact, she works here in this Casino.'

'What! Who is your daughter?' asked Ruby, giving him her full attention now.

'Nisha. I believe she works in surveillance.'

'Oh my God! Nisha. Of course, I know her. But she never mentioned that you were her father.'

'That's not surprising. I told you, we were not on good terms. Maybe, I shouldn't have spoken about us, either.'

'Don't worry. I don't gossip. Your secret is safe with me.'

'Thank you.'

'You know what, you have cheered me up. Let me give you something in return.'

'I don't want anything. I am happy that you accepted my apology.'

'No, I insist. Try your luck at Table 38.'

Kumar Saurabh laughed.

'Don't laugh it off. I am serious. Even Balwant won a few rounds on that table.'

Kumar Saurabh swallowed his drink in a single gulp and stood up.

'Thank you. But, why me? Why are you giving me this tip?'

'I told you, you cheered me up,' Ruby smiled.

Kumar Saurabh shook her hand and headed for Table 38.

Ruby turned her attention back to Balwant, who was now falling all over the craps table, throwing his money away. Another hour or two she figured, and he would lose all that he had won earlier. She wondered why he drank so much. Tonight, it wasn't her bad luck rubbing on him, it was the alcohol doing the damage. She sighed, thanked the bartender, got off the stool and turned to leave. But someone grabbed her arms from behind. The grip was so hard that she almost screamed.

'Not so fast, darling,' said Anton. 'Spend some time with us too.'

'You are hurting me!' she said. angrily. 'Let go!'

'Oh! I am sorry. I didn't know your kind are so delicate,' he said sarcastically, letting her arms go.

'What do you want?' she fumed.

'I notice that your lover has been winning tonight.'

'Oh! One night he wins and you are twisting my arms! You had no problems when he was losing all these months! I don't remember getting any appreciation or bouquet of flowers.'

'Don't you be cheeky now,' he replied, irritated. 'Make sure that he doesn't leave the casino until he has lost it all.'

'Fuck off. You don't tell me what to do.'

'You do have this habit of pissing me off,' he said, grabbing her arms tightly again and squeezing them hard. A current of pain ran through her entire body and she tried to free herself from his grip. But he was too strong for her. She was in agony, but there was no way she would give him the satisfaction of seeing that. She stared back at him stonily.

He pulled her towards him. 'I can do this all night, sweetheart,' he said laughing. 'How long will you resist!'

'Let me go, you bastard.'

He squeezed her arms even harder. 'So much attitude. I love it.'

Ruby realised that unless she gave him a sense of victory, he would not let her go.

'Okay, I'll go sit with him,' she said quietly, as if she had lost the will to fight.

Anton grinned, but continued to hold her arms in his iron grip. 'I didn't hear that,' he said. 'What did you say?'

'Let me go. I will do as you say,' she said.

'That's better,' he replied. Blood rushed through her arms as he released his grip. 'Darling, next time it won't be your arms, it will be your neck,' he whispered as he walked away.

Ruby's arms were bruised where he had gripped them and she rubbed them gently to ease the pain as she walked slowly towards the craps table. She heard Anton laughing behind her. Furious, Ruby decided that Balwant would leave the casino a winner tonight no matter what it took. Anton's behaviour had only strengthened her resolve. He would never have the pleasure of walking all over her, whatever the cost.

SMILE, LIKE YOU JUST HAD A LEAK

Louis, the blackjack dealer, was taut with tension. He tried to smile. He even cracked the customary jokes with the regulars. But it was clear that he was doing all this mechanically. Louis was usually a cool customer. Under normal circumstances, he dealt hundred-thousand-dollar hands without blinking. But today, his beloved son was on the line.

His unusual behaviour had not gone unobserved. Nisha was the first to notice the beads of sweat on his forehead. She had looked closely at him early in the evening. Luckily for Louis, he wasn't doing anything wrong then. Thus, she had lost interest in him after a few minutes of trying to decipher any patterns.

Anton was also watching him from a distance, hoping that he wouldn't crack under the pressure. He had his own plans for the evening. The continuing pain in his toe was a constant reminder of the thrashing he had received from Jesse and his gang. His ego had been bashed, and he was planning to get his revenge. If he allowed the incident to pass, it would send the wrong signal—that he was weak—and embolden them further. They couldn't be allowed to get away with this. On that day, he had been surprised and having been outnumbered, had no choice but to give in. But today, they were on his territory. He had prepared his lockup the previous evening, rearranging the chains that hung from the ceiling. They were ready to hoist two souls; which two, the evening would decide. Tonight, he was the one who would lead the game.

As the clock approached the midnight hour, Louis began to sweat profusely. He kept looking at his watch. Finally, when it was ten minutes to twelve, he gestured to the Pit Boss that he needed to take a toilet break. Within minutes, a new dealer appeared at the table. Louis handed over to him and made his way towards the designated toilet. Around the same time, Jesse entered the casino with the twins, Fatso and Baldy.

Anton, who was keeping a close watch on the entrance, jumped when he saw Jesse enter the casino. This wasn't part of the plan. He wasn't supposed to be here. Why the hell did he have to come himself? Jesse used to be a road side drug peddler. He had risen through the ranks as Goa transformed from a backpacker's heaven to a leading entertainment and holiday destination of South Asia. There was hardly any user of the white powder who had not crossed his path sometime in his life. There was bound to be somebody here who would recognise him.

Then Anton saw Baldy follow Jesse and smiled grimly. How could he forget the face that had bagged him? Jesse wasn't to be touched, but no promises had been made about providing a safe passage to his cronies.

Five minutes later, Jesse and his goons entered the designated washroom for their rendezvous with Louis, who was waiting for them anxiously. The twins immediately went to work, checking to make sure that they were alone. Once they gave the green signal, Jesse walked over to the man washing his face at the sink. He whispered his name to Louis, who immediately turned around to face him with folded hands, begging for his son's release.

'Stop it,' yelled Jesse. 'Unfold your fucking hands and stand up like a man. You can't be seen begging us.'

'I will do as you desire,' said Louis in a broken voice. 'Let my Pinchoo go.'

'Do your bit and Pinchoo will be back home before you finish your shift.'

Baldy pulled Louis into the water closet, shutting the door behind him. He pulled up the left trouser leg to reveal a neatly hidden card dispenser taped to his knees. A card dispenser, also known as a 'shoe' in casino parlance was used to hold cards after they had been shuffled. Casinos used a six-card or an eight-card deck dispenser.

'This is a six-card deck shoe like the ones you are using tonight,' said Baldy. 'As you must have figured, the cards are pre-arranged.'

He unbuttoned Louis's jacket and hid the shoe under his arm. Then he opened the door of the washroom stall and told Louis to walk out.

'Can you see anything boss?' asked Baldy, as Louis walked out of the water closet.

'Nothing at all,' said Jesse. 'It's all good.'

'Now, get your composure back,' said Jesse. 'Smile, the "after taking a leak" kind of smile.'

They all laughed.

'Walk back to Table 51 and replace the existing shoe card with this one,' instructed Jesse. 'Leave the original shoe card under the table on your left.'

'But, how?' asked Louis. 'The cameras will catch the switch.'

'Don't worry, it's been taken care of,' replied Jesse. 'As soon as you make the switch, we will join the table.'

'What if some of my regulars decide to join the table?'

'They won't. There are only three seats on Table 51, which we will occupy.'

'Now hurry, we don't have much time. Let's get your son back home.'

Louis walked to his table in the casino. He gestured to the Pit Boss that he had returned. Table 51 was empty.

Under normal circumstances, his action would have raised eyebrows as it was the duty of the Pit Boss to allocate specific tables to dealers. But Louis was an old timer and the Pit Boss decided to overlook his impudence.

Louis immediately went to work on the table, pretending to organise the chips while he surreptitiously looked around to ensure that no one was watching him. Then he stared at the camera above the table. If the camera was on, then the switch would be caught and security would be all over his table within minutes. He prayed to the Almighty and quickly replaced the shoe of cards on the table with the one hidden under his jacket. It was done in a blink. Then he dropped the original shoe of cards under the table and put his left foot on it. Now there was nothing left to do, except wait for the three men to join him.

Meanwhile, Mr Chadha who happened to be loitering nearby decided to make his life more interesting by plonking himself on one of the seats. Louis had suspected that something like this would happen. This would spoil everything. He had to take immediate action.

'Excuse me, sir,' he said. 'But this table is closed.'

'I am in no hurry,' replied Mr Chadha . 'You will open in some time, won't you?'

Louis was desperate and in no mood to be kind and gentle. 'Sir, you don't understand,' he said firmly. 'This table is already taken. If you wish to play, kindly move to one of the other tables.'

'I don't see anyone here,' said Mr Chadha, getting agitated.

Luckily for Louis, Jesse and his two sidekicks were coming towards the table.

'Sir, there they are,' he said, looking relieved as Jesse walked over.

But Mr Chadha was in no mood to leave. Jesse immediately took charge and threw a 10,000-rupee chip at him for his trouble.

The chip did the trick and a happy Mr Chadha moved quickly to another table. Jesse made himself comfortable on the chair at the centre of the table. Baldy, who had earlier assisted Louis with the card shoe, sat on his right and Fatso occupied the chair on his left.

Jesse took out a bundle of notes and asked Louis to exchange them for chips. Louis got busy counting out the chips and Baldy, who was sitting on his left, immediately bent down pretending to tie his shoe laces and in the process picked up the original card shoe from under Louis's foot and taped it back to his leg. He had practised the operation many times, and it was done with such finesse, that none other than those already in the know figured what had transpired.

Louis handed the chips to Jesse and to the other two customers. Now they were ready to play. The cards were pre-arranged. In the first three hands, Jesse and the guy sitting to his right would win. In the fourth hand, they would all lose to the dealer. Thereafter, every alternate hand would be won by them. So, the game wasn't a complete throwaway. But, since this pattern was known to the customers, they threw some lose change when they were to lose and went on a rampage when they knew that they were going to win. Jesse figured that in another half an hour, they would have more than doubled what they were owed by Anton. Ideally, at that point of time, they should call it a day and leave.

Greed grips the heart and binds the soul. It is difficult to leave when the going is good. When you know that you are going to win for certain, it is impossible to leave. With every successive win, they became more undisciplined. Anton watched them from a distance. He knew that they were testing the limits of their luck. He wanted Jesse to win more than his fair share. Only then would Jesse overlook what he was going to do later that evening.

I WILL CHANGE YOUR LUCK

She knew what she wanted—to get Balwant out of the casino before he threw away all his winnings. But how was she going to do it? He had come to the casino feeling that this was his lucky day. Winning all that money on Table 38 had made him feel even more invincible. He believed that he was on a roll tonight. Why would he quit when the going was so good? But for the past two hours he was consistently losing at the craps table.

Getting Balwant to leave would be difficult enough; to add to it, Anton had put up his own roadblocks. She would have to sneak Balwant out when Anton was distracted. She looked at Balwant with feigned disinterest while her mind raced to find a solution.

Then an idea struck her and she turned to look at Table 38. Kumar Saurabh was warming up. She hoped that the table would prove as lucky for him as it had for Balwant. If Kumar Saurabh began to win, then he would go on a rampage turning the casino upside down. All she had to do was wait. When the noise on Table 38 became louder, it would attract the attention of the crowds as well as the security. That would be the moment when she could slip out with Balwant. If Balwant agreed to be led out, of course. At present, he seemed to be in no mood to leave.

Balwant threw the dice again and the crowds cheered him on, shouting his name repeatedly. He was thrilled. Here he was a gambler like all of them. It didn't matter that he was not an urbane, English-speaking, sophisticated socialite, so long as he had the money and was willing to throw it into the game. He didn't care whether he won or lost.

Ruby moved closer to him, rubbing her body against his. But he did not notice.

'Darling,' she whispered, biting his ears. 'I have the first night out in years to go out with you. The anticipation is killing me.'

'What's the hurry, baby,' he replied in a slightly slurred voice. 'The night is long. I am just warming up.'

'That is exactly my worry,' she said aloud. 'By the time you down enough whiskies to be warmed up here in the casino, you will have gone all cold where it matters.'

Balwant laughed aloud. 'Those are the problems of the rich and fashionable. Us village folks, we have no such problems. We have kept the flag of India's burgeoning population flying high all these years.'

Ruby was irritated at this pointless conversation. He was drinking like there was no tomorrow, and with every drink, his gambling grew more reckless. If she didn't act fast, it would all be over soon.

In desperation, she began to nag him to leave. When even that didn't work, she began to pull on the sleeves of his shirt like a child tugging at its mother's saree. But this was going too far and Balwant scowled at her to stop pestering him. He held her arm and gently pushed her away. Ruby gasped. He had inadvertently touched the very spot that Anton had so cruelly bruised. Bewildered, Balwant immediately let go of her arm. One look at her face told him that something was wrong. 'What happened, darling?' he asked, concerned and rolled over the sleeves of her dress before she could stop him. He was shocked to see the large, angry bruise. The faint imprints of fingers were also visible. His eyes blazed with anger. 'Who did that?' he demanded. 'Give me a fucking name.'

The only thing worse than a drunk Balwant was an angry Balwant, and this one was both drunk and angry. He had lost interest in the game. He was looking for a fight. If she gave him Anton's name, he would punch Anton into oblivion. Which was exactly what she didn't want. She had to act fast before he attracted the attention of every soul on the casino floor. 'Shushshsh!' she said, putting a finger on his lips and pulling him away from the craps table.

Meanwhile, Table 38 had begun to get noisier with every spin of the wheel. Kumar Saurabh was raking in money and people thronged to the table to get a piece of the action.

'I am all right,' said Ruby, making light of the wound.

'No, you are not,' he said tersely.

Ruby looked away from him and her eyes hunted for Anton. Where was he? Then she saw him hovering around Table 38 at the other end of the casino floor, staring down at Kumar Saurabh, who was now on a roll. This was just the opportunity she had been waiting for.

Turning back to Balwant, she said, 'I am fine.' Before he could say anything, she put her hand on his mouth. 'Listen to me,' she said. 'This argument can wait. These things happen every day to us. This is part and parcel of our life. Who all will you pick a fight with?' She looked into his eyes. He seemed to be calming down. She moved her hand from his mouth and continued. 'I have seen you lose money on my watch for the past two years and I have felt so guilty for it. Tonight, I am not going to let it happen again. We will walk out of this casino while you are still winning. I will not allow you to ruin your life.'

Balwant had never seen Ruby like this before. He was pleasantly surprised. He looked concerned and amused at the same time. 'Cool down, baby,' he said, putting his hands on her cheeks. 'Why didn't you tell me earlier that you felt this way. We would have left much earlier.'

'Earlier! What did you think I was trying to do for the past two hours? But you were more interested in losing money than making love to me. All you have done is lose at that craps table.'

'Ok darling, I hear you. Just one last throw of the dice, and we are out of here.'

'Well, let's get on with it, then,' she replied.

They walked back to the craps table. He took out a chip from the mound of chips kept in front of him and handed it over to Ruby.

'What are you doing?' She asked.

'I have been playing with my profits all this time. With this chip in your pocket, even if I lose every chip on this table, we will still end the night on a winning note. Isn't that what you want?'

'You are crazy,' she replied, slowly smiling.

'You already knew that,' he grinned, as he picked up all the chips kept in front of him and bet them on a single number. The crowd gasped, ladies bit their nails, the Pit Boss ran his fingers through his hair in tension and the dealer stared in tense anticipation.

'Darling, aren't you going to wish me?' he asked.

Ruby kissed him on the cheek and closed her eyes as he threw the dice. She heard the sound as it hit the table and then rolled and rolled, finally hitting the corner of the table. Then there was silence.

She slowly opened her eyes and couldn't believe what she saw. It was snake eyes! The crowd erupted in euphoria and the Pit Boss pulled his hair in horror. Balwant had won! He had won on her watch!

He turned around to her. Tears of joy rolled down her cheeks. He gave her a tight hug and kissed her. He continued to hold her as their lips parted, still gazing into her eyes. The world melted away around them. Then he kissed her again and the crowds cheered.

'Didn't I tell you, darling, that I would change your luck,' he slurred and raised his hands in the air gesturing to the Pit Boss to call it off.

The Pit Boss immediately went to work encashing his chips for cash. They waited for him to return, standing by the bar staring at each other. No more words were exchanged. Ruby was still keeping a sharp lookout for Anton. She knew that it wasn't over until they were out of the casino. Balwant saw Karishma strolling on the casino floor and called out to her.

'Karishma, didn't I tell you that Ruby was my lucky charm,' he said.

'You have won?' she asked.

'A bag full,' he replied. 'I told you that I know my diamond.'

'Congratulations! You are full of surprises.'

'The surprises have only just begun.'

The Pit Boss returned with a suitcase full of cash. Balwant and Ruby walked out of the casino holding hands, escorted by two men from security carrying the suitcase.

A motorboat took them to the shore where a limousine waited to carry them to Balwant's hotel.

Once they were in the car, Ruby sighed with relief. Her eyes shone with joy. She hadn't failed him tonight.

THANK YOU FOR FORGIVING ME

Kumar Saurabh had decided to fully exploit Ruby's tip. Not for himself, but for his daughter. Whatever money he won tonight would go to her. As for himself, he had already decided on a great goodbye, the kind that was fit for kings.

It had taken him just a few minutes to figure out that the wheel of the roulette table was unbalanced, thus giving rise to non-random results. With the odds in his favour and borrowed money in his pocket, he made the most of this once in a lifetime opportunity to rake in the money. Typically, his histrionics at every win attracted more crowds to the table. Some came to try their luck by imitating his actions. But most came to look at him put on the finest act of his life.

The noise also attracted Anton and Nisha to the table. Anton was literally breathing down Kumar Saurabh's neck, but Nisha maintained her distance from her father. Anton didn't know why Kumar Saurabh was winning so consistently, but Nisha's sharp eyes quickly spotted the problem with the wheel.

She wondered what she should do. Exploiting an unbalanced table wasn't exactly a crime, but, in such cases, many casinos refused to pay the entire amount, negotiating a lower pay-out. The person now winning at the table was her own dad. This was so bloody awkward. She didn't want to be the one pulling him away from the table. She thought for a minute or two, time during which Kumar Saurabh continued to win, and decided that it would be best to tell Anton—not about her father, but about the table. When she pulled Anton away from Kumar Saurabh and told him about the unbalanced wheel, he asked, 'Are you sure?'

'Yes,' she replied.

'Then what are we waiting for?' he cried. 'We must shut the bloody thing down.'

'But, it's not illegal,' she argued.

'Legality, my ass,' he yelled. 'We are losing money every second here.'

Nisha walked away to the centre of the casino, while Anton rushed to the table and gestured to the dealer to stop the game. She heard the crowds booing as the game came to a halt. Then she heard her father's familiar voice abusing everyone and their mothers. It was as if a toy had been pulled out of the hand of a child.

Nothing was worse than shutting down a game when a high-roller was on a winning spree. Kumar Saurabh created enough ruckus to ensure everyone knew it. He made sure that he came across as the victim. Everyone liked to back the underdog against the house and thus, there was no dearth of support or sympathy for him from the crowds who continued to boo Anton, the bad man who had shut down a lively game. Some even went to the extent of shaking Kumar Saurabh's hand and patting him on his back in a feeling of camaraderie. The more money they had lost at the casino, the more they felt that he was their champion, the lone warrior who was unbeaten against the house. Anton began to lose his cool. He pushed some people in the crowd who got too close to him and a brawl seemed imminent.

Just then, Jayesh arrived on the scene. One look and he had grasped the situation. He placated Kumar Saurabh and calmed down Anton. Kumar Saurabh had not been a superstar for nothing and he brought his considerable acting skills to playing the victim perfectly, arguing his innocence. Jayesh tried to shepherd him to his office to discuss the matter, but the star knew that he needed the support of his audience and insisted on thrashing out the matter right there on the floor of the casino. Finally, though both Jayesh and Anton knew that Kumar Saurabh wasn't as innocent as he claimed to be, they had to give in and accept his version that he had won all the money fair and square.

However, Jayesh was a master negotiator and Kumar Saurabh had to agree to give up at least some of his winnings, though he kept a large part of it. He also agreed to give up his right to play at the casino that night. As he strolled off with his bag of chips held tightly under his arm, his audience dispersed, and Jayesh and Anton went about their work. Kumar Saurabh was looking for Ruby. He wanted to share his winnings with her. She was the one who had tipped him off and she had to be thanked. But Ruby was nowhere to be found.

After looking around for her for a few minutes, he went to the cashier and encashed his chips. He paid for a locker at the premises and locked all the money in it. Then he went over to the bar, took out a fancy cigar from his pocket and ordered a whiskey on the rocks. He pulled out an envelope from his jacket pocket. In it was a letter he had written to Nisha earlier that day. It was a good bye note. He pulled the letter out from the envelope and added a few words at the end.

I don't know if I deserved it, but thank you for forgiving me.

He replaced the letter inside the envelope, dropped in the key of the locker and sealed it. Calling over the bartender and asked him to leave the envelope with the concierge. It was to be handed over to Nisha at the end of her shift.

Now, there was nothing else to do. He sat there enjoying his whiskey and smoking his cigar with an air of satisfaction, no longer feeling the weight of his past on his heart. The guilt of being a bad husband. The guilt of being a lousy father. All of it was gone. His daughter had forgiven him. In one moment of kindness, she had released him from an evil spell that had sucked all joy out of his life. He also felt useful. For the first time he would be able to help her when she needed something. This was the perfect ending to a life otherwise spent on selfish pursuits. He had no further desires. There was only one thing left to do.

He finished the whiskey in one large gulp, stubbed the cigar and stood up to leave. Just then, his eyes fell on someone he never expected to see in a place like this. He smiled delightedly. This was the icing on the cake, the only thing missing from an otherwise memorable evening.

'Jesse,' he called out.

HER WORLD STARTED TO UNRAVEL

Once they were in the limousine, Ruby's excitement quickly subsided and anxiety started to rise. The smile vanished from her face. She wondered when and how she should confess the truth about herself to Balwant. How would he react? Would he reject her? Would he be hurt? Furious? *All three*, she thought miserably. Would he physically abuse her, kicking her in the stomach and punching her on the face? She recalled horrific accounts she had heard from other *kathoey*s who were beaten by drunk customers who felt humiliated when they discovered their true identity. She turned to look at Balwant. He was sitting in a corner of the limousine, holding her hand and humming happily to himself.

'I told you darling, I will change your luck someday.'

No. This man couldn't hurt her. She was sure he wouldn't ever raise his hands at her. But that didn't mean that he wouldn't be disappointed, or upset. After all, she had lied to him all this while about who she was. How could he ever trust her? How could she convince him that she loved him? That her feelings for him were real and deep?

It is true that in the beginning he was a client and she was his escort. But she had thought of him and treated him as a lover for a long time now, watching over him when he was drunk and vulnerable, even crying at night when he lost money on her watch.

Would he give her a patient hearing? More importantly, would he believe her? Or would the night end in despair, she being thrown out on the road as soon as he discovered the truth? She hoped and prayed that he would recognise the reality and depth of her love that extended beyond the physicality of this world. She hoped that it was strong enough to withstand this blow. She hoped for a miracle.

'We have reached,' said Balwant, breaking into her gloomy thoughts.

She looked at him searchingly.

'What's the matter, darling?' he asked

'Nothing,' she replied, shaking her head.

'Don't worry,' he smiled. 'I am a gentleman.'

She smiled wanly as they got out of the car and took the elevator to the penthouse. It opened into a large living area with plush interiors and glass walls overlooking the city of Panaji. The view was stunning. But Ruby hardly noticed it, her thoughts wandering elsewhere.

The seating in the room was organised in two areas, one centred around the television and the other around the bar. Balwant guided her towards the bar.

'Make yourself cosy as I change into something more relaxed,' he said, and walked into the adjacent room dragging the suitcase behind him. For someone who slurred every time he spoke at the casino, his mind and speech seemed remarkably clear.

She removed a duffle bag lying on the sofa and made herself comfortable. She needed to calm her mind. She picked up the magazine kept on the table in front of her and began glancing through it, but gave up after a few minutes. She could not focus on anything. The same thoughts kept playing in her mind like a tape recorder on a loop.

When a few more minutes had elapsed and he didn't emerge from the bedroom she began to wonder if he had passed out.

'Darling, are you alright?' she called out.

There was no reply. Balwant was taking a shower and hadn't heard her.

The wait was killing her. She began to pace up and down in the room. She wanted to open the door and peek into the bedroom, but she didn't want to embarrass him. What if he was busy counting the money? She decided to make herself a drink to calm her nerves.

The bar table was adorned with many bottles of Chivas 18. Ruby recognised them. It was the only alcohol that Balwant drank. Every time he visited the casino, his bottle came with him.

She opened the cork from one of the bottles and poured herself a large drink. Leaning against the bar, she took a small sip. A puzzled look appeared on her face. She took another sip, then another. Finally, she drank the entire amount.

What the hell! She picked up the bottle and examined it closely. There was nothing wrong with it. It was a regular Chivas 18-year-old with 40 percent alcohol. She pulled out the cork and sniffed at the contents. It smelled like whiskey.

She decided that she was so tense that even her taste buds had gone into nervous shock and stopped working. She poured herself another large drink and downed it in one go.

What the fuck! She stared at her glass again and as realisation dawned, her world started to unravel before her eyes. Questions came crowding into her mind. Questions to which she had no answers. She didn't understand what was happening. Had she been taken for a huge ride? Anger began to build up inside her.

YOU HAVE WALKED INTO A TRAP

Kumar Saurabh was drunk and loud as he called out to Jesse. Many people heard him, but most ignored him. Not Anton. He swung round when he heard that loud voice and looked at the table where Jesse was playing.

Jesse simply pretended he had not heard his name being called.

'Boss, did someone call out to you?' asked Fatso.

'Yeah, I heard it too,' he replied.

'Do you know who it is?'

'I have no idea. I don't intend to turn around and look unless I have to.'

Louis heard this conversation nervously and stopped dealing.

'I had nothing to do with this,' he pleaded.

'Who said anything to you,' snapped Jesse. 'Continue dealing, the guy may give up.'

'Doesn't appear so,' replied Baldy. 'He is walking towards us now.'

'Oh God! We are going to get caught,' said Louis, his voice and hands trembling.

'Shut up!' said Jesse. 'Control yourself and all will be fine.'

'Jesse, my friend,' the voice called again, louder than before. Kumar Saurabh had covered half the distance between the bar and their table.

'Shit! I don't think we have a choice,' said Jesse, angrily. 'We will have to call this game off. Fatso, you go and get the chips encashed. I'll take care of this person.'

'What about me, boss?' asked Baldy.

'You continue playing for a few more minutes. I don't want all of us to suddenly abandon the table. Once you see us walking out of the casino, make a quiet exit.'

Then Jesse looked up at Louis. 'You my friend, will continue to deal as if nothing has happened. Not a word to anyone. Play your part and I promise your son will be back home.'

Anton, who had been waiting all evening for the right moment to set his plan into motion, knew that the time had come for him to act. He saw Fatso leave the table and make his way towards the cashier with the chips. But Jesse was still there.

Jesse stood up and turned around to face the person calling out his name. When he saw who it was, his anger blew away; he smiled with pleasure and went forward with outstretched arms to hug Kumar Saurabh.

'Do you have some powder on you?' asked Kumar Saurabh loudly.

'Shushshsh!' said Jesse, as a few people looked up. Then he whispered, 'Of course, I do, my dear old friend. But not here. It is in my car.'

'What are we waiting for? Let's walk out,' said Kumar Saurabh.

The next moment they were walking out of the casino, their arms round each other's shoulders. This was the moment Anton had been waiting for. He immediately buzzed Nisha.

'I don't like Table 51. Ask Jack to put a spotlight on it.'

Anton and Jack never spoke to each other. Their egos could never be accommodated in the same room. Therefore, it wasn't uncommon for Anton to pass messages to Jack through Nisha.

'Why? What's wrong with Table 51?'

'I don't like Louis's body language.'

'That's funny. I felt the same way earlier in the evening. I watched him from a distance, but there seemed to be nothing wrong and I moved on.'

'Did you consult with Jack before making up your mind?'

'No. I didn't,' she replied.

'Then do it immediately.'

Anton had a fair idea about what would happen next. He casually walked towards Table 51 with a grin. He wanted to keep an eye on Nisha as she dialled Jack. But he wanted to do it from a distance, not making it apparent. He knew that there was no recording for Table 51. It was one of the new tables mentioned in the blackout list—the same blackout list which Jack had tried unsuccessfully to confirm with him. Had the camera on the table been on, the surveillance team would have caught on to the act much earlier. Since he hadn't heard from them all this time, it meant that Jack had complied with the list.

Nisha dialled Jack. Anton couldn't hear her but the expression of shock on her face pleased him immensely.

'What do you mean, the camera is switched off?' she said.

'I was told to switch it off in the evening before the opening,' replied jack.

'Told by whom?' She sounded concerned.

'Anton. Who else?'

She looked up immediately, her eyes searching for Anton on the casino floor. Anton had turned away from her and was watching Table 51. Nisha looked at him and said, 'This is not looking good, darling. You have walked into a trap.'

'My instincts told me that something was fishy when I saw that list. I even tried contacting that son of a bitch, but he didn't respond.'

All that is history now,' she replied, her mind racing to come up with some defence. 'Tell me, how did Anton communicate with you?'

'The same way as he always does. When I arrived in the evening, there was an envelope waiting for me at my desk with the enclosed list.'

'That's great. So, we do have the list, don't we?'

'No, we don't. I destroyed it after giving the requisite instructions. We never leave a trail.'

'Shit. Leave whatever you are doing and find Boss. Tell him what has happened. You have to convince him that you had nothing to do with this.'

'I didn't.'

'I know that darling, but it looks very bad for you.'

'Aren't you panicking? He hasn't even found anything amiss at the table. He has a hunch. What if the hunch is wrong?'

'Darling, you are so naive. Do you actually think that the list asking you to switch off the camera was a coincidence? I am sure that there is something going on at that table. Besides, knowing Anton, he will have me discover it.'

Jack regretted not contacting Jayesh earlier that day. If only he had spoken to him about the change in the blackout list, all would have been well. He should have never trusted Anton.

'You are right. I better go look for Boss. What about you?'

'I have no option but to play his dirty game. I have a horrible feeling that this evening will not end well.'

YOURS TO TELL

Balwant was standing at the bedroom door watching her. 'You are right,' he said. 'It is not alcohol.'

Ruby swung around to face him. 'I don't understand,' she said.

'It is a bottle of whiskey, but it contains only coloured water.'

'But you have been drunk on this for the past two years.'

'Darling, I was drinking this, but I wasn't ever drunk.'

'This makes no sense. I have seen you sway and slur with my own eyes.'

'All part of an act...'

'An act?' She was speechless, trying to make sense of what he said. 'Oh God. I need a real drink,' she said.

'Please help yourself from the minibar,' he replied. 'I don't drink.'

'What else don't you do?' she asked, anger bubbling up and threatening to spill over. 'It seems I don't know you at all.'

'That is harsh. You do know me well.'

She glared at him as she went to the minibar, pulled out a miniature bottle of scotch and downed it in one go. This time the spirit left a trail of warmth all the way down to her stomach.

'I don't know if anything is real any more. You did lose all that money, didn't you?' she asked sarcastically, staring at him again. He smiled at her and her anger erupted. 'I have lived in guilt for the past two years, even crying at night when you lost money. Answer my bloody question, did you lose that money or not?'

'It's not quite so simple.'

'Say yes or no, goddammit!'

'Well, if you insist on an answer, I did lose that money. But it wasn't the way you think.'

'Nothing seems to be the way it looks with you. Did you meet me accidentally, or was that part of some grand plan too?'

'You can never win or lose too often at a casino without arousing suspicion.'

'But you lost for two damn years.'

'Yes, I did. Why do you think I got away with it without attracting attention?'

'Ha-ha! Because you had the perfect alibi. You were in my company, the queen of bad luck. How could anyone question your loss.'

Balwant nodded. 'You are finally getting the drift,' he said.

'Oh! I am getting much more than that. What was I thinking all this time? You are so stupid and naïve, Ruby. It was always too good to be true. Oh God, how did I allow myself to fall into this?' She rubbed her eyes and said, 'Balwant, I am tired. I would like to go back.'

'Not yet. You aren't finished. Just tell me what is bothering you the most.' Balwant's voice was gentle.

'Tell? What more is there to tell? You have made a complete fool of me. And I am scared of asking what else I have missed seeing. I have had enough.'

'Don't be afraid. Ask.'

'Do you love me? Oh, why do I even ask? That must be some elaborate game as well.'

'What do you think?'

'I don't know, I don't know anything anymore.

Balwant walked up to her, pulled her into his arms and kissed her passionately.

'Do you still need an answer?' he asked

Ruby was confused. She should have pushed him away, but she did love him so very much. Except that now she wasn't even sure who he really was. She was quiet.

Balwant gently lead her back to the sofa and sat her down beside him. 'Okay,' he said. 'I'll tell you everything. It is true that our first meeting was not accidental. But I soon fell in love with you. I tried to tell you so often that my loss at gambling was not because of you. I kept telling you that there is no such thing as bad luck, that one day, I would change your luck.'

Ruby listened quietly. She wanted to believe him, but she was still unconvinced.

'I can't take this anymore,' she said. 'I have to go now.'

'Wait! You are not going anywhere till I finish. Don't you want to know why I wanted you at the hotel tonight?'

Their eyes met but she said nothing.

'Did you really think it was about sex? The only way I could ensure that they gave you your passport was by calling you to the hotel. You do have your passport, don't you?'

'Yes,' she said uncertainly, not sure what he meant.

'Pick up that duffle bag lying on the carpet. It belongs to you.'

Ruby looked at the duffle bag. She remembered moving it from the sofa when she had sat down earlier.

'Come on. Open it.'

She opened the bag. There was an airline ticket, a sim card and a wad of US dollars.

'Two hundred thousand,' said Balwant, when she looked at him questioningly. 'Enough money for you to make a fresh start in your country.'

It took Ruby a minute or two to take this in, then she looked at him and tears filled her eyes.

'Why are you sad now?' he asked. 'Isn't this what you always wanted?'

She dropped the bag and held his hands.

'Yes, there was a time when all I wanted was money. But that was before I met you. What will happen to us? I can't imagine living a life without you. And, oh God, I don't even know who or what you are anymore!'

He kissed her cheek.

'Yes, you do know. In your heart you know. And I have no intention of living without you. I will get in touch with you as soon as things cool down a bit. Keep that sim card carefully. I will call you on that number.'

Ruby should have been jumping with joy, but now all her fears and apprehensions came crowding back. She had to tell him the truth about herself. Would he still want to give her the money and come to meet her after that? Or would he just throw her out of his room and never want to see her again? For a few seconds she toyed with the idea of not telling him the truth. She could just leave quietly now and address this issue when she had got that all important sex change operation done. In fact, he need never know at all. But would she be able to live with herself knowing that she had been so deceitful with her lover? Ruby knew that it was not an option at all. She loved him and she would be honest with him and take the consequences.

'I have a confession to make too,' she said.

'Darling, what is it? Can't it wait?'

'No, it can't wait. It has already waited too long. I should have confessed much earlier, but I was selfish and weak. I didn't want to lose you.'

'Baby, what is it?'

She took a deep breath, held his hands and looked him in the eye.

'I am a ladyboy.'

She waited for the reaction as the seconds passed. She waited for him to pull his hands away, spit on her face, push her away. Instead, he smiled and pulled her closer into an embrace and gave her a peck on her forehead.

'I know,' he said. 'I have known for some time.'

She was thunderstruck. She had imagined all kinds of responses but not this one. 'How did you know?" she asked.

'It is not important.'

'Why didn't you confront me earlier?' she asked.

'It was not for me to confront you. It was for you to tell me. I was waiting for the day you felt comfortable and secure enough with me to be able to let your guard down. You had to realise that our love was strong enough to withstand this.'

The tears that she had held back for so long spilled out and he hugged her tightly.

'I am sorry, I didn't tell you earlier. I was so afraid of losing you.'

'It is alright,' he said. 'I love you for who you are. Nothing else matters.'

'I have dreamt of being a woman from the day I was old enough to realise that I wasn't. I am going to fulfil that dream now.'

'Do as you please. Do what makes you happy. But don't do it for me, for I love you the way you are.'

'Thank you,' she replied.

'Now, you better get going, lady. There is a taxi waiting for you downstairs that will take you to the airport. There is an early morning flight to Mumbai. By the time they realise at the casino that you are missing, you will be on your flight to Bangkok.'

She hugged him as she picked up the duffle bag. They left each other a parting kiss before she disappeared into the elevator.

Ruby walked hurriedly out of the elevator towards the waiting taxi. She didn't notice the large group of villagers waiting in the lobby with their bags packed and ready to go. Had she paid more attention, she would have seen the familiar faces of people who usually cheered Balwant at the craps table.

She got into the taxi, while the villagers waited for their ringleader to arrive.

NOTHING WILL GIVE ME MORE PLEASURE

Anton moved closer to Table 51 and stood opposite Louis. He wanted Louis to see him watching as he dealt the cards. He knew how nervous that would make him. Under that kind of heat, they all broke down. It was only a matter of time.

He grinned as Baldy pretended to play the game undeterred. He was not going to let him go. Not without settling scores and letting it be known that he wasn't to be messed with again. Since they had already walked away with huge winnings, he figured that they wouldn't mind losing a little to indulge him. Baldy was a professional and would never divulge any names. So, he could beat the shit out of him all night, confiscate his winnings and earn brownie points with Bobby and Jayesh.

They were fools to have come to his castle to play. The camera above the table might have been switched off, but there were enough cameras in the casino that would have caught their faces. Especially the one at the cash counters. It would have definitely caught Fatso encashing the chips. Anton intended to keep the investigations under his control and use it as leverage in his dealings with the drug mafia.

As for Louis, a few slaps across his face and he would narrate his life story. Anton had no interest in him. All he wanted was Louis's confession that the surveillance team had been compromised. Then he could finally tighten the noose around Jack's neck. Jack would be the biggest prize of the night.

He turned around as Nisha walked up to him.

'Did they find anything?' he asked innocently.

'Nope,' she replied, her eyes staring at him, trying to pierce through his web of deceit. 'The camera was switched off.'

'Switched off! But why?'

'You tell me!' she said, angrily. 'It was on the blackout list that you sent him.'

'Says who? Your pretty boyfriend? I did no such thing. Why didn't he raise the matter earlier, if there was a change?'

Nisha didn't want to argue with Anton. She realised that Jack was on a weak footing. He had walked into an ambush. She had little choice but to play along.

'What do you propose, we do?' she asked.

'Let's take them for questioning. We don't have evidence, but the fact that the camera was also switched off sounds shady to me.'

'Looks like you have already made up your mind that they are guilty.'

'I haven't yet, but if I get evidence that something fishy has happened, then I will spare no one. I mean no one. That includes your boyfriend.'

Nisha didn't need him to tell her that. Anton sounded very confident and she knew that evidence was waiting to be found. She wondered if Anton knew of their plans to leave the casino and go to Singapore.

'Let's finish this,' she said, walking towards the table and asking Louis to call off the game.

'Stop the dealing? Why? What happened?' asked Louis, his voice shaking.

'A hunch. For all you know, it is nothing. We need to ask you a few questions.'

Baldy, who was sitting at the table pretending to be indifferent to what was happening around him, stood up to leave.

'I better move to a new table,' he said.

'Please sit down, sir,' said Nisha. 'I need to ask you a few questions too.'

'Me?' said Baldy, looking surprised. 'Why? What have I got to do with all this?'

'No reason for you to get worried, sir,' Nisha replied. 'It's part of the process, you see.'

'I am not worried,' he said. But he was, both worried and tense.

Nisha turned round to face Louis while Baldy grabbed the chips in both his hands and ran for the exit. Anton had expected something like this to happen and had positioned himself a few metres away at a vantage point. As a result, Baldy didn't get very far. Anton tackled him from the side with such momentum that they both flew in the air. For a man who was relatively short at five feet eight inches, Anton packed quite a punch. What he didn't have in height, was more than made up for in width. He was like a battering ram. They both fell on the casino floor with a loud thud. The chips flew out of Baldy's hands. The next moment, Anton had pinned his head to the ground with his entire body weight on top of him.

'You are not going to get a word out of me,' gasped out Baldy, grimacing.

'I am counting on it,' replied Anton, with a devilish smile.

Security surrounded the spot within seconds. Anton continued to sit on Baldy, one of his knees pressing his head against the ground, even though it was no longer required since they were surrounded by security men. But this was Anton's idea of fun. It was only when Jayesh reached the spot and pushed through the crowd that Anton finally let him go and allowed two security personnel to hold him by the arms.

'What happened?' asked Jayesh. 'We are attracting too much attention.'

'This person made a dash for the exit,' replied Anton.

'Frisk him,' ordered Jayesh to one of the security personnel.

As soon as they frisked Baldy, they found the card shoe taped to his leg. A triumphant smile lit up Anton's face.

'Oh! You have made my day!' he whispered in Baldy's ears.

'Which table was he playing on?' asked Jayesh.

'Table 51,' replied Anton.

Jayesh immediately turned around to look at Table 51. Louis had broken down and was being consoled by Nisha, as two security personnel held him by his arms.

'Louis!' said Jayesh in disbelief. 'Good job, Anton. I want you to get to the bottom of this.'

'Nothing will give me more pleasure, Boss,' Anton replied as the security personnel escorted Louis and Baldy to the lower deck of the ship.

Things had gone better than Anton had envisaged. He had not expected to catch Baldy with the card shoe on him. Now he could do as he wished with him without anyone raising a finger. It was time to put his second act into play. Louis would confess in no time. Not his guilt—that Anton had no interest in—but about the complicity of the surveillance team.

Nisha was so caught up in the happenings, that she had almost forgotten about her earlier talk with Jack. When the security took Louis and Baldy away, she saw Jack standing at one corner of the room and she rushed to him.

'What happened?' Jack asked her.

'That was Anton's plan coming to fruition. Tell me that you spoke with Boss?' she prayed.

'I couldn't. Things happened so fast,' he replied.

'Darling, what have you done?' she cried.

'I can still speak with him.'

'It is too late now. We will have to take our chances.'

Jayesh walked to the open deck of the ship to get some fresh air. He lit up a cigar and thought through all that had happened so far. He wondered what else lay in store before the night ended. He couldn't imagine Louis being involved in a fraud. The guy had dealt for a decade to the highest rollers. Never had anyone raised an eye on his conduct. Why the hell had such a man got involved in a fraud?

Also, the player seemed familiar. *What are you up to Anton?* he wondered.

TIME TO SHOW HER CARDS

Jill sipped her margarita and looked at her watch for the umpteenth time. She had been sitting at the bar for nearly a couple of hours, chain-smoking and downing margaritas, observing the people and happenings around her. In particular, she had kept a keen eye on Karishma, the journalist.

Karishma was the central figure in the execution of her plan. It was Jill who had sent her the unmarked parcel a few weeks ago, setting the stage for an enquiry into the ownership of the casino. Jill had also mentioned in the note that Karishma must find a way to get herself invited to the inauguration of the new casino if she wished to unravel the case. Therefore, Karishma had immediately accepted Jayesh's invitation.

Jill had a single point agenda on her mind for the evening: she wished to meet Karishma. She knew that cold leads without a name or a face didn't go very far. There was always the suspicion that there was malice in their intent and that they were being used to lead the enquiry in a particular direction.

But her case would be bolstered if she met the journalist face to face and identified herself as the person behind the allegations. Putting a face to the story would give the necessary confidence to the journalist to pursue the matter.

But, her chance interaction with Ruby earlier that evening changed everything. There was no doubt in her mind that the kinky VIP under discussion was none other than Pankaj Adhikari. She had harboured an intense anger and resentment against him for many years. She had kept a low profile, but she was a woman scorned looking for an opportune time to extract her revenge. Was this that moment? Could a deathly strike tonight crumble him beyond repair? This was the critical question.

She had dreamed of this day for a long time. Now, that the opportunity was before her, she felt nervous. In an ideal scenario, she would have been behind the scenes providing information to Karishma, who would have done all the necessary work. And Pankaj Adhikari would have never known who it was that had wreaked havoc in his life. But, if she decided to go ahead with the plan tonight, then she would certainly be in harm's way. She would have to lead the strike from the front, revealing herself. She didn't know how the day would end for Pankaj Adhikari, but there was a distinct possibility that she wouldn't leave the ship alive. Was it worth risking her life? The answer was clear in her mind.

What life? she wondered. *I don't have a life. I have been hiding behind shadows all these years. I have nothing to lose.*

It was tonight or never. Her mind made up, she took a deep breath, stood up from the bar stool and made her way towards Karishma, who was standing a few metres away from her. The clock showed 1:00 am. She figured that she should wait for another 45 minutes before striking. *Let the action warm up a bit before I crash the party,* she smiled to herself grimly.

'Hello dear,' she said, surprising Karishma, who was looking curiously at the melee in front of her.

'Did that man just dive tackle that bald guy who is now pinned down to the floor?' asked Karishma. 'Or, are my eyes playing tricks on me?'

'No tricks, darling,' replied Jill. 'Some poor bastard cheated and made a run for it when he got caught.'

'Oh! Does this happen often? You don't look surprised.'

'You will find all kinds of drama playing out in a casino. Nothing surprises me anymore.'

'Hmm! I should visit this place more often. Jill, please tell me some interesting gossip. You have a reputation to maintain.'

'Ha-ha! Sure. Now which one should I tell you…? I once saw a guy pick up a handful of 5000 buck chips from a high-roller's table, shove them inside his pants and then rush to the exit. The security blocked all the exits so he crashed out of the window into the river below.'

'What happened?'

'What do you think? The poor guy was caught. There is no easy way out of here.'

'Why do you call him 'poor guy'? He was a thief, wasn't he?'

'Well, it's a matter of perspective. Stealing from a casino, which basically robs everyone else, is romantic. I called him "poor", darling, because I know very well what must have happened to him after he was caught.'

'What happens after they are caught?' asked Karishma in a whisper, her curiosity aroused.

Playing along, Jill moved closer to her and whispered in her ears, 'There is a dungeon in the lower deck of this ship. It is right out of the gory old thrillers, they tell me.'

'Wow! Can we see it?' asked Karishma, excitedly.

'Darling. I hope we never see it.'

'Oh-ho, just when it was getting interesting. What else have you heard about this place?'

'You are nosy, aren't you?'

'It is my job, you see. I didn't come here to admire fake boobs, chat up drunks, or throw some chips. I am here for a real story.'

'Real story! Like what?'

Like, who owns this place?'

'Jayesh does,' replied Jill, firmly. 'He is the boss.'

'Is he?' asked Karishma. 'I was hoping to get some juice out of you. Especially, as you come so highly recommended by none other than Jayesh Shah.'

Karishma knew how to play on people's egos. It always worked. But here, Jill was the one calling the shots and she played along.

'Jayesh is a friend,' she said, 'And I don't wish to talk loosely about him.'

'Whose talking about Jayesh?' said Karishma. 'I am enquiring about the ownership of this casino. Don't you worry about loose talk. Every lead that we get starts with loose talk. More often than not, where there is smoke, there is always a fire. Point me in the direction of the smoke.'

Jill pretended to let her guard down.

'Rumour has it that this place is owned by a powerful politician.'

'Now you are talking,' said Karishma. 'But I have already seen the ownership papers. They are all clean. Jayesh owns this place.'

Karishma was watching Jill closely and noted that Jill looked neither shocked nor surprised. She didn't bat an eyelid. Jill was pleased that Karishma had acted on her anonymous lead. But, if she didn't give her more to chew on, then it was likely that she would lose interest soon.

'Of course, he owns it on paper. You will have to dig deeper, darling. For such an acclaimed journalist, you disappoint me.'

Karishma's interest was well awakened now. *This woman knows more than she is revealing. I wonder who she is*, she mused. She decided to play dumb, coaxing Jill into letting out more information. 'I am at a loss. Where do I dig deeper?'

'You know, like how he had the money to buy this place? Or, who he bought it from?'

'I still won't find the name of the politician, will I?'

'I guess not. The papers are always good. But you should get clues. There are always telltale signs. Every time I see a rag to riches story which beats the odds, I know the real story is buried underneath somewhere.'

'Don't be so cynical. You have to give credit to the entrepreneurial spirit of the risk taker.'

Come on, darling, you have much more to tell me. My sixth sense is telling me that this is not a chance encounter, Karishma thought to herself.

'Dig deeper into the transfer of ownership. For such a large and successful establishment, there should be many suitors. These transactions are complex and cumbersome. They take time. But, in cases like this, they seem to happen rather suddenly, almost overnight. Jayesh could be gone tomorrow and someone else might take over the casino, like this,' Jill snapped her fingers.

'For a person merely gossiping, you are indeed insightful.'

Jill wondered whether this was the right time to come out in the open. She looked at Karishma, trying to decipher the expressions on her face. She had done her homework on her, and so far, Karishma hadn't disappointed. This girl was a crusader. She fought for the truth. She wasn't scared of anyone. Jill decided it was time to go all in.

'I was the one who sent you that anonymous parcel a fortnight back,' she said.

'I had a feeling it was you,' replied Karishma, with a smile on her face.

'My only protection was my anonymity. Now it is gone.'

'Don't worry, I never ever reveal my sources.'

'It is not that simple. If we decide to go ahead on this, then I will have to reveal my identity. That means putting my life in danger. Will you be able to protect me?'

Karishma, who was never easily disconcerted, was taken aback by the sudden seriousness of the discussion. She had never dealt with a life and death situation before.

'I will be truthful with you,' she replied, earnestly. 'I have never dealt with such a situation before. But I will do all in my power to protect you.'

They both looked at each other. No words were exchanged, but much was said.

'I believe you,' said Jill. 'I was the owner of this casino before it was transferred to Jayesh.'

'I didn't find your name in the transfer papers.'

'Oh! That's because my real name is Angela Da Rosa. I am the missing link in your story.'

'Tell me more,' said Karishma.

'We don't have time for that. But I have mailed you a packet before coming here. You should get it in a few days. Inside it, you will find the missing pieces to your puzzle, information that will help you nail that son of a bitch.'

'Ok, but at least pose for a photograph with me. It will add to the evidence.'

'Sure,' replied Jill, and they both stood together while the photographer clicked.

Then Jill glanced at her watch. Another 5 minutes to go.

'Are you ready for the grand finale?' she asked.

'What do you have in mind?'

'Nothing less than a Triple Sundae Chocolate Fudge.'

'I am drooling.'

'What are we waiting for? Let's see some live action then.'

'Lead the way.'

'Sure. Ask your photographer to follow us.'

Karishma had many questions but decided to go with the flow.

THERE WAS NO FIGHT LEFT IN HIM

The security team escorted Baldy and Louis to the lower deck of the ship. Anton had set up a replica of the 'interrogation' rooms that existed on MV Babbar. Despite having worked at the casino for over a decade, Louis had no idea about the hell that existed below the casino floor. On the lower deck, the two were taken into separate rooms. Baldy, a hardened criminal, showed not an iota of worry on his face, but poor Louis was on the verge of breaking down.

Anton left them alone for a few minutes before arriving at the lower deck. He first went to Louis. He was concerned about the old man. Louis was a simple guy who worked hard to make a living. He probably had never even jumped a red light in his life, and here he was, sitting in the dungeon, caught red-handed, not knowing what would happen to him next. He was the collateral damage in Anton's plan. Anton had specifically chosen him because of his simplicity and likeability. He knew that no one would believe that Louis was the mastermind of this plan. Hence, when the information about the larger plot emerged, fingers would be immediately pointed elsewhere.

'Turn on the recording,' said Anton, before opening the door. He found Louis sobbing in the room, praying to the Almighty for forgiveness, his arms cuffed to the table.

'Who the fuck put handcuffs on him?' he yelled. "He is no bloody criminal.'

One of the security guys rushed to uncuff Louis.

'Get him a cup of coffee.'

'I don't want coffee. Please give me a phone,' he begged.

Anton handed him his phone. Louis immediately dialled his son. The phone rang a few times and then he heard the familiar voice of his son, sounding a little drowsy.

'Pinchoo!' he exclaimed. 'Are you alright, Pinchoo? Are you home?'

'Yes, dad, I am fine. I was sleeping. Your friends took good care of me.'

Louis was immensely relieved. Pinchoo was safe. He stopped shivering and looked more composed.

Ask me anything', he said to Anton who had seated himself across the table.

'I have only one question,' said Anton. 'Why did you do this? Didn't you know that you will be caught by the cameras?'

'I didn't have a choice. They had kidnapped my son, Pinchoo.'

'You should have taken us into confidence,' said Anton.

'The thought did occur to me. But they told me that you guys were compromised. I was scared. I didn't know whom to trust.'

'What do you mean we were compromised?'

'I told them that the card shoe couldn't be switched. The electronic surveillance would catch it. But they told me not to worry, that the camera above the table was switched off.'

'What?' Anton pretended to be shocked. 'You sit here for a while, old man,' he said, as he walked out of the room.

'Tell me that you got all that on the tape,' he asked his security guy, who signalled a thumbs-up.

Anton was elated. At last, he had proof that could nail Jack. But, before he went to work on him, he wanted to spend some quality time with Baldy. He had been looking forward to this moment all evening. Baldy looked fresh. He would give a good fight.

'Hang him up in the lockup,' he ordered, and went to his room. He opened a bottle of *feni*, a local Goanese brew made from cashew, poured himself a liberal drink, lit a cigarette and settled down in his armchair.

Baldy was built like an ox. If he decided that he didn't wish to cooperate, it would not be easy. Hence, it had to be done intelligently, without arousing his suspicion. The security guys got him out of the room on the pretext of recording his statement and escorted him to the lockup. The lockup was camouflaged and not visible from outside. But a sixth sense told Baldy that all was not well. Suddenly, the calm man turned into a raging bull, taking his captors by surprise. His hands were still cuffed behind his back, but he used sheer body momentum to take two security guards down, slam dunking one of them on the floor.

Anton poured himself another drink. He could hear the commotion outside as six men went to work on Baldy. Bodies were pressed against each other in a match of raw strength as Baldy fought valiantly against the six who tried to pin him down.

'Tire the son of a bitch,' yelled Anton. 'No electric shocks.'

He wanted to take Baldy raw. They could have given him an electric shock and then dragged his limp body into the lockup. But there was no fun in that. He would be all flaccid when Anton went to work on him. He wanted him to be awake, he wanted him to be angry. Then he would slowly work on him, a jab here, another jab there, and break him down. Ensure that he felt every punch, every bit of pain.

The contest was evenly matched for the first few minutes as the six men couldn't gain any significant advantage over Baldy. But then he began to tire, breathing heavily as the exertion took a toll on him.

Meanwhile, Anton poured himself another drink, his third and the largest. He had come to understand the virtue of being patient. What was the hurry? Baldy wasn't going anywhere. A few more minutes and he would be hanging by his arms in the lockup. He relaxed in his armchair waiting for the noise to die down. Then he left for the lockup with the bottle of *feni* in his hand. It was the only place with no security cameras. He shut the door behind him as he entered.

Baldy was standing in the middle of the room with both his hands cuffed to chains which were tethered to the ceiling. He looked up as Anton entered the room. Their eyes met for a second. Then Baldy looked around searching for cameras.

'There are none here,' said Anton.

'You son of a bitch,' he yelled. 'You have a lot of balls to take me into custody.'

'You should have thought about that before getting caught red-handed with that card shoe up your ass. What the fuck were you thinking? Everyone saw that. Now, even if I want, I can't help you.'

Baldy went quiet for a while, mulling over what Anton had said. 'But still, there is no need for all this. You can pretend to be mad.'

Anton smiled at him. 'You are right, I could if I wanted to, but I won't.'

'Why?'

'You beat me inside my fucking house. Nobody gets away with that.'

'Have you fucking forgotten that you might own this place, but we own everything outside it.'

'I have thought through everything, Baldy,' said Anton, as the first volley of punches landed on Baldy's face.

'You are dead, man!' yelled Baldy.

'Still threatening,' laughed Anton, as he put the bottle of *feni* to his mouth and gulped a few mouthfuls. Then he put it on the floor and swung around like a spring which had just been released.

Bang! The jab landed on Baldy's nose and he shrieked in pain.

'You are misreading the situation,' said Anton. 'Otherwise, you would have been begging me by now.'

Now Baldy was no longer threatening. He wasn't even speaking any more. Anton was the one talking.

'I gave you guys an opportunity to make some money on my watch. But you decided to overstay your welcome. Not that I would have let you walk out, Baldy. You son of a bitch! I have kept awake at night planning for the day when I will have my revenge.'

'I have you all on the recorded tapes. If you even think of touching me outside, the tapes will be released to the cops.'

He gulped a few more mouthfuls of the *feni*. Then, he pulled out his favourite baseball bat and did a little dance inside the lockup before landing a homerun on baldy's left knee. The moment the bat hit the kneecap, Baldy let out a loud shriek which was heard all across the lower deck of the ship. First, his left leg gave in, followed by the right which could no longer support his body weight. Now Baldy was actually hanging in the lockup, with his body weight supported by the arms which were tethered to the ceiling. He kept moving from consciousness to unconsciousness, sobbing in pain.

Anton looked satisfied. He enjoyed breaking people down. There was no fight left in Baldy now. He left him hanging in the lockup and went back to his room, Then, he called two of the security guards and asked them to fetch Jack.

'Sir, what if doesn't cooperate?' asked a member of his team.

'Treat him like anyone else if he doesn't cooperate.'

THOSE WERE THE DAYS

Jesse and Kumar Saurabh took the motorboat to the docks where Jesse led the way to a parked Mercedes 500 SL.

'You have done rather well,' said Kumar Saurabh appreciatively as they sat inside the car. 'This is a beauty.'

'Boss, it is nothing compared to the one you drive. But, I agree, it is a classic nevertheless,' said Jesse, pulling out a joint from deep within the glove compartment and lighting it.

Kumar Saurabh sighed in satisfaction as they took turns to finish the joint.

Meanwhile, Jesse kept a keen eye on the docks. He saw Fatso emerge with a suitcase in hand and start walking towards the car. But the moment he noticed that his boss wasn't alone, he turned away and walked off in another direction.

The two in the car finished the joint and sat quietly for a few minutes. Kumar Saurabh finally broke the silence. 'I still remember the time when you used to deliver on a scooter.'

'That was a long time back, boss. I remember, your action movie had just been released. What was it called?'

Kumar Saurabh gave him a blank look. 'I don't remember,' he said. 'It was too long back.'

'The name is on the tip of my tongue,' said Jesse, trying hard to recollect. 'Yeah! *Dumdaar*. That is what it was called, *Dumdaar*.'

'*Dumdaar*,' said Kumar Saurabh aloud, as his eyes lit up. 'That was my last superhit.'

'Boss, I remember on one occasion I came on my scooter and kept going round and round the hotel, hoping to catch you alone. You were in the lobby, but constantly surrounded by people. Finally, it struck me that I should become one of them. I walked up to you, asked for your autograph and left the consignment on your chair. Mine was the last autograph you signed that day.'

'Hahaha! Yes, I remember. I was blown out for the rest of the day. In fact, I was late for shooting the next day. The producer was very upset with me till I shared some of the powder with him in my vanity van.'

There was silence once again as Jesse lit another joint and passed it on to his friend. Kumar Saurabh took a few drags.

'Those were the days,' he said, sounding nostalgic. 'All have forgotten me now.'

'I still remember,' replied Jesse. 'I haven't forgotten a thing. I remember your warmth, and I definitely still remember the extravagant tips.'

'You are good man, Jesse.'

SOMETHING VERY DARK

Jill walked purposefully towards the Presidential Suite followed by Karishma and Gopal, the photographer. From way down the corridor, she saw a lone man guarding the door of the suite. She knew him. His name was Shera and he had been Pankaj Adhikari's bodyguard for over a decade.

Under normal circumstances, she would be no match for him and nor would her accomplices. But she had the element of surprise on her side. She gestured to Karishma and Gopal to slow down their pace while she walked quickly towards him.

Shera was taken aback to see her. He wasn't expecting anyone, and definitely not Jill. Had it been someone else, it would have raised alarm bells and he would have immediately gone into a defensive mode. But it was Jill, their Jill, as they used to call her once upon a time. She was their lady with a heart larger than the moon, always looking out for them, no matter how small they were in the scheme of things.

She smiled warmly at him. 'You look good, Shera,' she said, patting his forearm affectionately. But her eyes were fixed on the flower vase kept on a table behind him.

'I wasn't expecting you,' he replied, smiling back at her. But he was tense. He was uncomfortable and unsure about how exactly to respond to her. She needed to act fast before his discomfort turned into suspicion.

'You know, your boss, he is so unpredictable,' she said, trying to pre-empt the questions arising in his mind. 'I was at the party upstairs and I guess he found out.'

'Did he call you?' he asked.

'Yes. Why else do you think I am here? You can confirm if you like.'

'Don't misunderstand me, Jill. Your word is good for me.'

'But you don't look convinced,' she said, raising her eyebrows a little haughtily.

'You see, I am in an awkward position. I don't know how to say this, but there are already two women inside the room.'

'Jill smiled. 'This isn't the first time, is it? I guess it will be a foursome tonight.'

The tension visibly eased and Shera looked relieved.

'You know, boss is crazy,' he said. 'And you also entertain his requests.' He shook his head.

Jill smiled a little ruefully. 'Now, don't keep me waiting,' she said.

Shera pulled out the key from his pocket, turned around and bent to put it into the lock. For the first time his eyes were not on Jill.

Jill moved surprisingly fast and, in the blink of an eye, picked up the flower vase from the table and smashed it on Shera's head. The vase shattered into pieces and Shera fell on the floor with a thud. The noise brought Karishma and Gopal running towards the suite. Inside, the porn playing on the large television screen was so loud that Pankaj Adhikari had no inkling of the events outside the room.

'Was that necessary?' asked a shocked Karishma.

'This is no time to ask questions, darling,' replied Jill. 'Is your camera ready,' she asked Gopal.

'I am always ready,' he said.

'Don't be a smartass. The moment I open that door, you will get the best shot of your life. Make sure you make it count.'

Gopal turned on the flash as Jill turned the key in the lock. She gently pushed the door ajar the peeked inside the room. The door opened into a sitting room, which was unoccupied. There was noise coming from the bedroom. She went inside, gesturing to Karishma and Gopal to follow her. Once they were inside, she locked the door behind them.

They walked towards the bed room. With every step, the noise became louder. From the door of the bedroom, a part of the bed became visible.

Upon it lay a woman, stark naked, covered in nothing but gold paint from head to toe. She had her back to them. Her hands and legs were tied together in a tight knot behind her back, making it extremely difficult for her to move. They couldn't see her face. When Jill stepped further into the room, she saw that her mouth was gagged with a piece of cloth and she wore an expression of shock and horror. It took Jill no time to realise that the horror was at what she was witnessing.

Pankaj Adhikari was forcing himself on another woman who was spreadeagled naked on the bed, her arms and legs stretched wide and tethered to the bedposts with a rope. She was also painted in gold. Her mouth, too, was gagged. She shrieked and cried, but with her mouth gagged, her voice was just a gurgle. She was choking and in agony, tears rolling down her cheeks. This aroused Pankaj Adhikari even more causing him to work harder on her delicate, petite body.

Jill had seen some bad things in her life, but this violation of the human body horrified her. This was no orgy whose purpose was to give pleasure. This was no love, nor lust either. This was something very dark, an attack whose only aim was to inflict physical and emotional pain on the human body. This was extreme exploitation and violation of the human spirit. It stank of raw power and dominance.

Jill, Karishma and the photographer stood there shell-shocked for a few seconds. Then Jill exploded in anger.

She pulled off her high heeled sandals and hurled them at Pankaj Adhikari. The first one hit him on his butt; he was so busy violating the poor girl that he didn't react. But, the second one flew past his face, missing his eyes by a whisker. He turned his head and looked at the three standing there dumbfounded.

BUFFOONS JUST FOLLOW ORDERS

Few things go unnoticed in a well secured casino. The Presidential Suite was particularly well monitored. As soon as Jill broke the vase on Shera's head and entered the presidential suite, alarm bells rang in the security department. Within seconds, Jack was viewing the security footage. He had no idea who the VIP was who occupied the suite. All he knew was that a person guarding the room had been assaulted by a woman, and three people had entered the room.

As per protocol, he immediately dialled Anton. But, for the second time that night, Anton refused to answer his call. This time Jack even dialled his cell phone, but there was no response. Given his experience earlier that evening, Jack didn't take it as a case of oversight, but of intent. He immediately dialled Jayesh's room, but there was no response from there either. Obviously, he was still socialising on the casino floor.

'Keep an eye on that room and alert security,' he told one of his juniors as he rushed out. He had just reached the lift to go up to the lobby, when he heard someone call him. He turned round and saw Anton's security guys behind him.

'Boss wants to see you,' said one of them.

'He is not my fucking boss,' replied Jack, turning back to the lift. 'And where the hell is he? I have been calling him myself.'

Jack turned back to the lift, but one of the men came around and stood in front of him. 'He wants to see you now in the basement,' he said, firmly.

'What the hell is this?' cried Jack angrily. The man behind him grabbed arm.

'Get your fucking hands off me, you arseholes,' he yelled in frustration.

'Mr Jack, don't make this more difficult for yourself,' said one of them, and gripped his shoulder.

Jack realised that something was terribly wrong. Struggling was futile, so he calmed down. These buffoons were only good at following orders. There was no point in talking any sense into them. 'Oh ok, take me to him then. I need to talk to him urgently anyway,' he said giving in.

He noticed that a few of his staff were looking out of the control room. They looked too scared to come to his aid. Should he tell them to inform Jayesh about the incident at the Presidential Suite, or should he save his own ass first? He figured the latter was more important and there was only one person he could bank on.

'Tell Nisha,' he yelled as the two men yanked him into the lift.

By the time Jack reached the lower deck of the ship, Bobby was already there. He had spent a few moments speaking with Louis, who had narrated the story to him about the online surveillance being compromised.

Anton was playing this by the book. He wanted to make sure of his ground before he took on Jack. Even he understood the severity of what he was about to do. Challenging Jayesh's authority behind his back was one thing, but to beat up one of his key people was quite another.

Jack saw the accusing look on Bobby's face. He was bewildered. This wasn't good. He hoped that someone from his team had reached out to Nisha. She was his only hope. But he had to give her time to act.

'What the hell is all this?' he demanded angrily. 'Why have I been dragged here like an accused?'

'You aren't an accused yet, but you might as well be,' replied Bobby. 'All the evidence points to you.'

'What are you talking about?' asked Jack.

'Give me one minute with him, he will remember everything,' Anton said, raring to go at Jack.

Bobby ignored him and continued to address jack. 'We caught a cheat a few minutes back. The blackjack table was rigged. The dealer was compromised and so was your team.'

'My team? What do you mean?'

'We have a confession from Louis, the blackjack dealer, that your team was hand in glove in the act. The camera above the table was switched off. Only you could have given such an order.'

'I did give that order, but only because I was told to. I had an envelope on my table, like every day, listing the camera numbers that were to be shut down.'

'You slimy bastard,' yelled Anton. 'Boss, he is trying to wriggle out of it. Let me do it my way,' he begged again.

'Wait,' replied Bobby. 'Jack, when more tables were on the list, didn't it raise any suspicion in your mind?'

'It did raise a doubt! I even called Anton, but he didn't take my call. Then, I let it go; I didn't want to interfere in your business.'

'I am a busy man,' shouted Anton, agitated. 'I don't sit around here to take your calls.'

Jack continued, 'Whenever there is an emergency, I always call up Anton. I did in the morning, like I did a few minutes earlier. But it seems Anton is busier than usual today. He didn't pick up my call either time.

'Wait a minute,' said Bobby. 'Why did you call him a few minutes earlier.'

'Must be to save his ass, boss,' said Anton.

'Shut up, Anton, let me speak,' said Bobby.

'Finally, someone wants to hear what I have to say,' said Jack, knowing well that Anton was getting more and more riled. 'Someone broke into the Presidential Suite.'

Bobby, who had been composed through this entire interaction, was thrown completely off gear at this piece of news. He looked horrified and fearful. 'What? Why didn't you say so before?' he yelled.

'When did you give me a chance? And these buffoons wouldn't listen to me,' replied Jack, staring at the two security personnel holding him.

'Come on, Anton,' said Bobby, rushing towards the door. 'We have no time to spare.'

Anton stood there looking confused. 'What about him?' he asked, staring at Jack.

'This can wait.' Bobby was already out of the door and Anton ran to catch up with him. There seemed to be something seriously amiss.

'Who is the occupant of the Presidential Suite?' he asked.

'God,' replied Bobby.

'You lucky son of a bitch,' Anton yelled at Jack as he made his way out. 'I will break your teeth when I return.'

Jack heaved a sigh of relief. For the moment, he was safe. He prayed that Nisha would be here before Anton returned.

I AM CONVINCED OF YOUR INNOCENCE

Nisha knew that something was very wrong as soon as she saw one of Jack's boys come running towards her in the casino. Members of the online surveillance strictly stayed away from the casino floor.

'Catch your breath,' she said. 'Where have they taken him?'

'To the lower deck,' he replied.

Nisha bit her lips. She knew that people who spent even a little time in the rooms on the lowest deck could come out broken, both physically and psychologically, some not fit to even carry their own weight on their legs.

She had to find Jayesh and find him fast. Jack was mentally very strong, but he wasn't physically built to take abuse. She was worried that he wouldn't break psychologically and that would give Anton the excuse that he so desired to break him down physically.

Jayesh was not in the casino. Her urgency caught the curious gaze of many customers. She wondered where he could be. The last she had seen him was with Anton right after the blackjack incident. Perhaps he had retired to his room. She immediately went to the administrative wing and ran towards

Jayesh's chamber and pushed the door open. This was no time for formalities.

Jayesh was sitting at his desk, putting papers into a briefcase. His secretary of many years, Lisa, was standing beside him. He looked up as the door opened and a panting Nisha rushed in. He gestured to her to catch her breath.

'Make sure that it is kept in my car,' he told Lisa, who walked out with the briefcase. Then he turned to Nisha, and asked, 'What happened?'

'Anton's men have taken Jack to the lower deck against his wishes.'

'The son of a bitch. How dare he?'

Jayesh picked up the phone and dialled Anton, but there was no response. Anton was, at that moment, on his way with Bobby to the Presidential Suite.

'Let's hurry down. It isn't too late,' he said.

'How do you know? asked Nisha, her hopes rising again.

'He would have taken that call had it been too late. Either he hasn't finished what he desires, or he isn't there at all.'

A minute or two later, they reached the lower deck of the ship. The security personnel were shocked to see Jayesh. They had only run into him on the casino floor. He was always calm and dignified. But the Jayesh that they encountered today had eyes blazing with anger and the force of authority in his manner. He might no longer be what he used to be a decade earlier, but an old lion is still a lion. He was clearly in command and they were trained to obey.

A couple of them hesitantly stepped forward as if to block his way, but one furious look and they quickly stepped back. It was only when he reached the door of the interrogation room that they actually tried to prevent him from entering by forming a human chain around him.

'Where is Jack?' he yelled. 'Is he inside?'

'Yes sir, he is,' said one of them. 'But we have orders to not let him go under any circumstances.'

'Step aside, I am here to talk to him,' ordered Jayesh.

'Right, sir,' heaved the head of the team in relief. They moved away and let Jayesh and Nisha enter the interrogation room to meet Jack. One of them radioed Anton to tell him of Jayesh's arrival on the lower deck.

As soon as the door opened, Nisha ran to Jack and hugged him hard. She ran her hands all over his body to see if he had been hurt.

'I am fine, darling,' he said. But she continued to move her hands, stopping only when she had completely reassured herself. She looked up at him. Jack smiled, and said, 'Am I glad to see the two of you!'

In her panic, Nisha had forgotten that Jayesh was in the room, still standing by the door. She turned back and looked at him, embarrassed.

'He appears to be okay,' said Jayesh. 'You made it in time. Now let's figure out how to get you out of this hellhole.' Jayesh pulled out a chair. Jack and Nisha sat across him.

'Tell me what happened.' said Jayesh.

Jack narrated the events of the evening.

'Did you try to reach Anton?' asked Jayesh.

'Yes, I tried,' replied Jack. 'But I couldn't reach him.'

'Why didn't you call me?' asked Jayesh.

'I told you,' said Nisha, jumping into the conversation. 'If only you had done that, all would be fine.'

Jayesh gestured to Nisha to calm down and allow Jack to speak.

'Boss, in retrospect, that was the ideal thing to do. But, at that moment, I felt that I was being too cautious in raising the issue. Our last conversation about facilitating the business was still on my mind. I didn't want to be seen as an unnecessary pain in the ass.'

Jayesh thought quietly for a few seconds.

'I know you are innocent,' he said, as he got up from the chair. 'Now let me get down to some work.'

'Boss, I am not leaving his side,' said Nisha.

'Ok, you two remain here. Let me get hold of Anton and sort this out.'

'How will you convince him?'

'I will tell him the truth—that I knew,' said Jayesh, smiling.

CAUGHT IN THE ACT

'Who the fuck is that?' yelled Pankaj Adhikari, without moving an inch. He still lay on top of the poor woman, his lard filled belly crushing her petit body under its sheer weight.

'Darling, I came to give you a surprise,' said Jill. 'You always said, "the more the merrier", remember?'

Pankaj Adhikari recognised the voice and turned. His eyes took in Jill, Karishma and Gopal with his camera behind her. His mouth and eyes opened wide in shock.

Gopal wasted no time. He went into a frenzy lighting up the room as if a strobe light had been turned on at a nightclub. This was like winning a lottery. Every newspaper in the country would beg for a piece of this action. Sex, sleaze and politics were a bestselling combination.

Jill hardly noticed the flashing lights. She dived onto the shocked Pankaj Adhikari much like the dreaded, shrieking kamikaze pilots during the second world war. Pankaj Adhikari did not react in time and Jill smashed into him with full force, her sheer momentum knocking him off from the girl, as the two of them tumbled to the floor.

'Missed me darling?' she yelled, sarcastically.

All the supressed frustration and anger of the past years came bursting out of her as she slapped and scratched Pankaj Adhikari's face. But Adhikari was no small man. Once the initial shock receded, he fought back, slapping her hard across her face.

Instead of helping Jill, Gopal did what he knew best, and kept flash illuminating the two of them as they pulled at each other's hair. Finally, Pankaj Adhikari realised that it was all being filmed and shoved Jill away and stood up panting. 'Bitch, I took care of you all these years, and this is how you return the favour?' he yelled. He wasn't prepared for a WWE match right after his interrupted orgy. Even a politician has his limitations.

'Took care? Don't make it sound like a good bloody deed! You did it to save your own ass. When was the last time you visited me? You didn't even know if I was dead or alive.'

'You are right. I made a mistake. I should have had you bumped off a decade ago.'

While they squabbled, Karishma untied the women. If these two girls could corroborate the photographs, it would make for an explosive story.

'What do you think you are doing?' demanded Pankaj Adhikari, when he noticed the women sitting up free of their bonds. 'We were only playing a game here. These girls were willing.'

'Ha! Is that what you are going to tell your voters?' said Karishma. 'I am not as naïve as them. Take one look at this poor girl's face and you would know that she didn't sign up for this.'

'Perhaps, I got a little carried away,' said Pankaj Adhikari, finally wrapping a towel around his waist. 'You still don't have anything. I, on the other hand, will sue you for breach of privacy.'

'Is that how you think this is going to play out?' Karishma untied the final knot and set the girls free. 'Time will tell,' she added as she found two bedsheets and threw them to the girls to wrap around themselves.

'You all get out of here,' yelled Jill, suddenly. 'Karishma, go.'

'I am not going anywhere without you,' said Karishma.

Pankaj Adhikari started laughing.

'None of you is going anywhere,' he said. 'Have you forgotten that you are in the middle of the river? You might have come here of your own will, but none of you is leaving without my specific approval.'

'I don't see anyone coming to your aid,' said Karishma. 'Unless you are counting on that poor soul lying unconscious outside.'

'Oh! Not him. This is a casino. Nothing goes unnoticed here. There should be people coming any minute. I am surprised that they aren't here already.'

As if on cue, Bobby, Anton and half a dozen security men burst into the suite.

'Come right in, Bobby, Anton,' called out Pankaj Adhikari.

'You know what to do, Anton,' said Bobby, as they walked into the bedroom.

Anton and his men confiscated all the mobile devices and Gopal's camera, their wallets, purses and all other personal belongings. Jill, Karishma and Gopal were now in custody. The two girls sat trembling on the side of the bed, the white bedsheets accentuating their bizarrely golden faces.

'How could you let this happen, Bobby? I am losing faith in your abilities.' said Pankaj Adhikari, angrily.

Bobby kept quiet as his mind raced to find answers.

'Who invited Jill to the party?' Pankaj Adhikari asked. 'This other woman, is she the journalist who has been enquiring about me?'

Bobby pounced on the opportunity to blame Jayesh.

'Boss, all invitations were finalised by Jayesh. I never saw the invitation list. As for this other woman, give me a minute to check her identity.'

He turned to Anton. 'Anton, bring all the personal belongings here.'

'Yes, boss,' replied Anton. But first he spoke softly into his mike. 'Under no circumstances should Jack leave the lockup,' he said. 'Is that understood? I am coming in a few minutes.'

Then he took the phones, camera and the wallets that they had confiscated to Bobby, who noticed that he looked upset and looked at him questioningly.

'Jayesh has gone to the lower deck. I need to get back. I am not letting that Jack walk out.'

'Okay. Leave these personal possessions behind and take the three of them with you to the lockup. Tell the boys to keep an eye on the two girls. They are not to leave this ship. Keep them in detention till we decide what to do with them.'

'What is this all about?' asked Pankaj Adhikari.

'Boss, we had an incident of fraud involving one of the dealers. Upon interrogation, he confessed that the online surveillance had been compromised. We are interrogating Jack, the head of online surveillance.'

'Hmm! There is too much going on tonight. But we must deal with this situation first. Anton, when you reach the lower deck, ask Jayesh to come here. Don't argue with him.'

Anton nodded and left.

LET THEM WALK

Anton's long held desire to have a go at Jack was on the brink of being fulfilled today. But, before he could smash Jack's nose into his eye socket, the son of bitch had deflected attention to the drama in the Presidential Suite. Now Jayesh had jumped into the fray and was in his den below the deck. This had changed everything. He rushed to salvage the situation.

Anton handed over Jill, Karishma and the photographer to one of his deputies and hurried to the interrogation cell where Jack was being held. He was relieved to find Jack still sitting there, but didn't notice Jayesh standing to one side of the room. He took a step back to catch his breath and organise his thoughts. But Jayesh had seen him and immediately confronted him.

'How dare you drag one of my people to the lower deck?' he demanded furiously. 'Have you forgotten your place in my casino?'

'Not at all, boss,' said Anton, taken aback. 'But all evidence points to him. We even have a confession. I have never had more evidence in the past.'

'Ha! You have shit and you know it. You know how easy it is to manipulate these things.'

'What are you trying to say?'

'Louis commits a fraud after a decade, only to get caught. All evidence points towards Jack. This is a fucking setup! The whole damn thing stinks.'

Anton began to lose some of his bluster and Jayesh knew that he had pushed the right button. Anton became more aggressive.

'Are you pointing fingers at me?' he asked.

'Not yet, I am not. Let Jack walk and all will be forgotten.'

Anton tried to hide his uneasiness.

'What! A few minutes earlier you were begging me to let him go, and now you seem to be threatening me.'

'I am not threatening you, but you have found nothing credible.'

'But I have.'

'Ok, let me burst your bubble in that case. Jack informed me about the extra camera on the list. I gave him specific approval to shut it down. I told him not to finger you for the sake of the business. I am the one you have to blame.'

'Boss, you might have many flaws, but I must say that you always stand up for your people. See how desperate you sound making up a cock and bull story to save that son of a bitch. Unfortunately, I am not buying your bullshit. I have him in my custody and I intend to squeeze the life out of him tonight.'

'Anton, you will do no such thing,' said Jayesh coolly and very firmly. 'He will walk out of this place.'

'Don't go all stern on me, Boss. If you want him out, you better convince Bobby about it.'

'Ok, if that's the way you want it. I will go to him right away. But, meanwhile, don't you touch Jack.'

'Oh! I forgot to tell you. This is the lesser of your troubles.'

'Why? What happened?'

'Jill played full drama tonight. She crashed into an orgy at the Presidential Suite and took that journalist and her photographer with her.'

'What the fuck! What's gotten into her? Who was the VIP?'

'The "Big Boss".'

Jayesh pretended to be shocked.

'What? Big Boss is here?'

'Yes, he is and he is screaming mad. He wants to see you immediately.'

'But I wasn't even aware that he was on the premises.'

'If it makes you feel any better, I didn't know either.'

'What are you going to do with the three of them?'

'I don't know. I am only following orders. I was asked to bring them to the lower deck and hold them here.'

'Ok. I'll go to the Presidential Suite. But no harm should come to Jack. I will have Bobby call you to let him go.'

As soon as Anton left the suite, Bobby went through Karishma's personal affects and pulled out her work identity card, press card and the driver's license.

'You were right, boss,' he said. 'She is a journalist.'

'Hmm! Just as I had suspected. The two of them are not here by chance. But there is always a silver lining. At least, now we can be sure that it wasn't the opposition gunning for my head.'

'That is a relief, indeed,' replied Bobby.

'You are still not out of the woods, Bobby. How did they find out that I was here? Find the answer while I get dressed.'

Pankaj Adhikari disappeared into the bathroom to change into something more dignified. He emerged after a few minutes looking calm and fresh as if nothing untoward had happened.

'Do you have an answer?' he asked. 'Who knew that I was coming?'

'No one but me,' replied Bobby.

'It can't be, think harder. This news has leaked to Jill from somewhere. Did Jayesh know about it?'

After a moment of silence, Bobby replied, 'The only other person I spoke to was Ruby, the head of our escort service, to organise the girls.'

'Did you mention my name to her?'

'Of course not, boss.'

'Hmm! Where is Ruby? It might be worth having a late-night coffee with her.'

Bobby remembered that Ruby was out with Balwant.

'Boss, she is on a client visit. I will organise a meeting with her as soon as she returns.'

'Ok. Tell someone to clean the phones and the camera. I don't want any data remaining on them.'

'I will get someone to work on it immediately.'

'Actually, on second thoughts, let me do it myself.'

Pankaj Adhikari took out the storage disk from the camera and smashed it with a paper weight. Then he went to work on the mobile phones, checking their photo gallery to see if any photographs had been taken. For a politician, he was very knowledgeable.

He nodded his head as he went through Jill's phone. In her anger, she had forgotten to take any photographs. She was so predictable, always emotional and stupid. She would pay for what she had done tonight.

Karishma's phone had a few photographs. He went through them, admiring himself, before deleting them one after another. Then he checked her WhatsApp and email to see if she had forwarded them before the phone was confiscated. She had attempted to send a WhatsApp message but it had failed to go through due to poor connectivity. For once, Pankaj Adhikari thanked the inefficient telecom service. He deleted the WhatsApp message.

Then he perused through her personal messages to see if she had any exchanges with Jill. But Jill didn't exist in her list of contacts. That was interesting. Perhaps, this was not as well planned as he had feared.

But, a few minutes later he found a few SMS messages that had been sent out an hour earlier. "I am on an undercover mission on the casino ship, MV Sultan. In case, I do not return to work, contact the police immediately and hold the entire management of the casino responsible."

'Bitch,' said Pankaj Adhikari, aloud. 'We will have to let them go. To be doubly sure, ask someone to clean these phones and the camera one more time. Then give them back with our complements.'

'What?' said Bobby. You are going to let them off?'

'We have no choice. This wasn't an impromptu act. This was premeditated action. She had informed people before coming here. People, who will be up our asses if she doesn't return.'

'Well, in that case I will make sure that the cameras are turned on to record their exit from the casino. But, once they are off this ship, she is fair game.'

'The journalist is not to be touched. There will be too much unnecessary heat before the elections, which I can do without.'

'But she can harm you.'

'She doesn't have any evidence. Make sure that both the girls disappear tomorrow.'

'What about Jill?'

'Oh Jill, she disappears too, but in small pieces.'

Bobby grinned.

'What about Jayesh?' he asked, with a big smile.

Pankaj Adhikari laughed aloud, trying to hide the surprise on his face.

Bobby had asked a pertinent question which had caught him off guard. He had plans for Jayesh, but under no circumstances was he going to involve Bobby in their implementation. He had other people to manage these things.

'Now, don't you get naughty,' he replied.

'I was joking, Boss,' replied Bobby, immediately realising his mistake.

'Now, where is Jayesh? He should have been here by now.'

I DON'T BELIEVE IN COINCIDENCES

Jayesh hurried into the Presidential Suite looking deeply concerned.

'Boss, I am shocked to hear about what happened,' he said. 'I don't know what got into Jill's head to do something so stupid. I wasn't aware that you were coming.'

He paused and pounced on Bobby.

'Bobby, why wasn't I informed that Boss was going to be here?'

'He was only following orders,' said Pankaj Adhikari. 'I wanted it to be discreet.'

'Boss, his laxity has cost us again. Why do you still stand behind him? He placed a single man to guard your room.'

Bobby wasn't going to take this lying down.

'This isn't the first time that Boss has made a discreet visit,' he replied. 'A single man outside the room makes it inconspicuous. It has always worked in the past.'

Jayesh wanted to argue but Pankaj Adhikari gestured to him to stop.

'The problem isn't the single guard, Jayesh,' said Pankaj Adhikari. 'The problem lies somewhere else.'

'What do you mean, Boss?'

'Who invited Jill?' asked Pankaj Adhikari.

'I did,' replied Jayesh. 'But I have invited her for every event during the past decade. I didn't see anything untoward in inviting her.'

'Who invited the journalist?'

'I did. But you both were aware of it. I had no inkling that she was acting in concert with Jill. I am as shocked as any of you.'

'How did they get to know that I was here?'

'I don't know, Boss. As I told you earlier, I myself was unaware that you were here, till a few minutes back.'

'Bobby tells me that the only person he spoke with was some woman called Ruby. She works for you, doesn't she?'

'Yes, Ruby works for me, as does everyone else on this ship.'

'Does Ruby know Jill?'

'She does.' Jayesh knew that all it would take was one look at the security camera footage to find out that he had met both Ruby and Jill together in the evening. 'I saw them hanging out together on the casino floor earlier in the evening.'

'So now we know how the information leaked,' said Pankaj Adhikari, smiling. 'This Ruby woman, I would like to meet her.'

'Bobby, was Ruby aware of who would be in the Presidential suite?' asked Jayesh.

'No, she wasn't. I only told her that a VIP guest had a particular request.'

'Boss, this doesn't add up. How could she have known that it was you?'

Pankaj Adhikari was losing his cool.

'These are matters of detail, Jayesh. The broad contours are clear. Information leaked from Ruby to Jill. Thereafter, they attacked me in my room. There is a link between the three of them. That link is you.'

There was a hint of a smile on Bobby's face.

'Boss, I had no role in this. I didn't even know that you were here.'

'I don't believe in coincidences, Jayesh. Maybe, you are speaking the truth. In which case, you are a very unlucky man, at the wrong place at the wrong time. But you will have to take a fall for what has happened tonight.'

'Boss, you have already made up your mind. I guess there is no point left in arguing. If you want me to go, say so. I worked here on your say so, I will leave, if that is what you desire.'

'Quite correct,' replied Pankaj Adhikari. 'It's time you packed your bags.'

Jayesh pretended to be hurt by the sense of urgency showed by Pankaj Adhikari. Actually, his bags had been packed a week ago.

'What will you do with the three of them?' he asked.

'That is not your concern anymore.'

'Boss, think through it with a cool head before you act. There could be repercussions.'

'I am aware of that, Jayesh. Thank you for your concern.'

'Out of curiosity, who will be taking over from me?' he asked.

'Bobby, of course.'

Jayesh looked amused, but he held his hands out to congratulate Bobby, who smiled triumphantly.

'I wish you well,' he said.

Both Pankaj Adhikari and Bobby relaxed. Jayesh had accepted his ouster without any drama or fanfare. Now was the time to ask them.

'One thing, before I leave,' he said.

'What is it?' asked Pankaj Adhikari.

'There was a case of fraud at the casino tonight. One of my men is being held on suspicion.'

'You mean Jack,' said Bobby. 'We have a statement against him.'

'Hear me out, Bobby, before jumping to any conclusions,' said Jayesh. 'You don't have a statement against Jack. The dealer has only confessed that the online surveillance was compromised. It could be anyone else.'

'What do you mean anyone else?' said Bobby. 'Jack is the head of the online surveillance. Only he has the authority to make that decision.'

'You are right that Jack has that authority. But he makes these decisions on the basis of recommendations received from your office. Frankly, you tell him what to do, and he does as he is told.'

'Oh! That is what he would have you believe. There was no recommendation from my office about that extra camera to be shut down.'

'How can you be so sure?'

'What do you mean?'

'Jack took my consent before shutting down that specific camera above the table on which the fraud occurred. I gave the approval without much thought, presuming that the request had come from your office and was communicated via Anton.'

'Are you suggesting that you were aware?' asked Bobby, surprised. 'How do I know you aren't lying to save his ass?'

'Why should I lie?' said Jayesh. 'Think about it. Jack is no fool to shut the camera and sit there drinking cola, waiting to be caught by Anton's men. Unless, he didn't know about it.'

Pankaj Adhikari and Bobby exchanged looks.

'Are you suggesting that someone wanted Jack to take the fall?'

'I am not suggesting anything, Bobby. These are things for you to find out. If Jack takes the fall, it will be an open and shut case.'

'Continue Jayesh,' said Pankaj Adhikari.

'Louis has dealt thousands of hands over the past decade, and there has never been an iota of doubt about his integrity. Today, for the first time, he committed a fraud and got caught, only to confess that the surveillance was compromised. Someone knew the inside working of our systems, exploited it to get the camera switched off.'

'I agree with Jayesh,' said Pankaj Adhikari. 'This needs more investigation before we can arrive at a conclusion.'

'Boss, I am worried that we might be shooting the messenger instead of the real perpetrator.'

'I will tell Anton to let him go,' said Bobby, hesitantly.

'If you don't mind, please call him now. Jack is already in a half coma. You have locked up a regular Joe.'

Bobby made the call. Anton's displeasure was audible through the phone. But it was done.

'Thank you,' said Jayesh.

Then he thanked Pankaj Adhikari for reposing confidence in him and walked out of the room.

AN END AND A BEGINNING

Jayesh strolled around the lobby of the casino meeting and greeting guests and employees alike. Despite all its ups and downs, the last 10 years had been amongst the best of his life. He had enjoyed the job that had been forced upon him, and though he had no regrets at leaving, he wished his exit had been a little more magnanimous. After all, he had given a decade of his life to the casino. He couldn't even tell the people he had worked with that he was on his way out. There was no farewell party to see him off. Then he shook his head. This was the best way to go—disappear like a puff of cloud and leave only memories behind.

After spending half an hour on the casino floor, Jayesh went back to his room. He wondered what would happen to Jill and the journalist. He also wanted to warn Jack and Nisha to get out of the casino and the state of Goa. Pankaj Adhikari's hands were long and far reaching.

Jack and Nisha were holding hands and waiting for him in his room. Jack looked tired and disturbed. He was an honest, sincere man who had encountered a world that was so out of the ordinary for regular god-fearing people. It was like visiting a police station for the first time. You didn't even need anything to happen to you. The whole environment is so caustic that it leaves an imprint on your soul, sucking the joy out of you. As soon as Jayesh entered the room, Jack stood up and shook his hands, thanking him profusely.

'If it wasn't for you, this day would have ended very differently for me,' he said.

'It's nothing,' replied Jayesh. 'In fact, I am the one who should be apologising to you, for letting you get into something like this.'

'No need to apologise. I couldn't have asked for a better boss. But, after what happened tonight, we have both decided to leave. We can't work here anymore.'

'I understand,' replied Jayesh. 'I would have felt the same way in your place. By the way, I am leaving too.'

'Oh my God! What happened? Did you take the fall for me? You shouldn't have done that.'

'No. This was long coming. Don't blame yourself for it.'

'So, what now? What will you do?'

'I haven't given it a thought. But first, I am going to disappear for a while, and relax on some beach. I suggest that the two of you should also get out of the city immediately.'

'Boss, we are both moving to Singapore. We plan to make a new beginning there.'

'That is great. But you don't understand what I am saying. Are your bags packed and ready to go?'

'No, not yet.'

'See, Anton, wasn't pleased to let you go. He will try to come after you again.'

'But I haven't done anything.'

'It doesn't matter. If he doesn't catch someone, uncomfortable questions will continue to be raised. So, you need to leave now.'

'In that case, we better hurry,' said Jack. 'I don't intend to go back to that shithole.'

'Don't worry, I will walk out with the two of you,' said Jayesh. 'But, once we are out of here, you make a run for it.'

'Sure, Boss,' replied Jack, and they all walked out to the elevator.

On the casino floor, Jayesh was immediately surrounded by regular customers and employees alike. He gestured to Jack and Nisha to wait a while as he met everyone and called it a night.

There was no reason to pretend that he was in charge anymore. Whenever an employee approached him regarding any operational matter, he redirected them to Bobby. It did raise a few eyebrows, but he didn't care. He met the old timers with a warmth reserved for long-lost friends. Some of them wondered what was the matter with him, but most assumed that it was a few whiskeys too many.

Jack and Nisha were waiting for him in the lobby when one of the senior cashiers accompanied by a person from concierge walked up to them carrying a briefcase, a gunny bag and a sealed envelope.

'What is this?' she asked.

'Ma'am, these were kept in our custody by Mr Kumar Saurabh with the instructions that they should be handed over to you.'

'Do you know what's inside?' she asked.

'No, Ma'am.'

'Ok, leave them here. Thank you,' she said.

She glanced at Jack. She wanted to look inside the briefcase. Jack read her mind and stopped her. 'Not now, darling,' he said. 'Let's get out of here first.'

She smiled and put the envelope in her purse and handed the briefcase and gunny bag to Jack. A minute later, Jayesh joined them and the three of them walked out of the casino together, on to a waiting motor launch that took them to the jetty. Had Nisha looked around, she would have spotted Kumar Saurabh's Ferrari in the parking lot. But she was in a hurry and didn't pay attention to her surroundings. Jack threw the briefcase and the gunny bag into the back of the car as they made their way to her house where she would quickly pack up her belongings and then they intended to drive out of the city immediately.

Jayesh got into his car and headed towards Mumbai. He was booked on an early morning flight out of India. He was not going back to his house. Pankaj Adhikari had let him go as a goodwill gesture, but he knew that his propensity for kindness could change at any moment.

WIN SOME, LOSE SOME

Bobby dialled a number in Panaji. The phone rang and rang, but there was no answer. He cursed and called again. This time a sleepy male voice answered the phone, a little irritated, 'State guest house, Panaji.'

'Son of a bitch! Are you asleep?' shouted Bobby.

The man recognised the voice and his eyes shot open and his mind came to attention. 'Not at all, Boss,' he lied. 'I was watching television inside. Please tell me, how can I be of help?'

Bobby gave clear instructions before slamming down the phone. The man wrote down the instructions on a piece of paper and then he went to work, pulling out a dilapidated client register from the reception desk in front of him. This wasn't the first time he was doing this job. He had learned from experience to leave plenty of space between client entries to accommodate VIP requests. These came at odd hours in the night without notice. There was an entry at

10:30 pm that night followed by another at 10:55 pm. He created a new entry in the name of Pankaj Adhikari at 10:45 pm, allotting him one of the VIP rooms which were always kept unoccupied for such requests.

Once the entry was made, he called Bobby to confirm that his bidding was done, and went back to sleep.

'Boss, your alibi is solid,' Bobby informed Pankaj Adhikari.

'Where do I have to go?'

'The State Guest House at Panaji.'

'Couldn't you come up with a better place,' complained Pankaj Adhikari. 'That place is infested with rats and cockroaches.'

'Boss, that's the only place which still functions without a CCTV camera. Please make sure to have breakfast in the dining hall so that some people see you in the morning.'

'Oh God! I will have to eat that watery sambhar with idly. Now get me out of here quietly.'

A few minutes later, Pankaj Adhikari had left the casino through a side staff entrance. Bobby had ensured that the relevant security cameras were switched off. Once he was gone, Bobby headed below deck to meet Anton.

Anton was upset. 'When the opportunity came to nail the sons of bitches, you went all soft', he complained.

'Why? We still have the two who were caught red-handed.'

'Oh, small fry! You let Jack walk away! He was the biggest catch of the evening.'

'Jayesh claimed that Jack had told him about that extra camera. Your story didn't add up.'

'He was lying through his teeth.'

'Even if he was, it wasn't a battle I wished to fight. I lost the battle, but won the war instead.'

'What! Is Jayesh out?'

'Yes, he is gone. From this moment, we rule this place.'

'That is great news, Boss! But I am still disappointed about letting Jack walk away. I really wanted to beat the shit out of him for a long time.'

'It is ok, we win some, we lose some,' said Bobby. 'But I will personally lead the investigation into this fraud to figure out what happened.'

Anton's excitement immediately disappeared.

'Why do you want to involve yourself in these small matters?' he said. 'You will be busy establishing yourself as the new CEO over the next few weeks. Let me handle it. You take care of more important things.'

Bobby noted Anton's eagerness to take over the investigation. 'Thanks, Anton,' he said. 'But you must keep me updated about your findings and progress.'

Nisha and Jack made quick stops at each of their houses and packed essentials and valuables and set off for Bangalore. It was still dark when they crossed the border of Panaji. Nisha had booked an evening flight out of Bangalore. They would have to drive the whole day to make it in time.

In all the rush of packing and leaving, Nisha had forgotten about the stuff that her father had left for her. It was only after they had crossed Panaji that she remembered the envelope in her purse. She pulled it out, opened it, took out the letter inside and began to read. With every passing word, her expression became grimmer. Finally, she said, 'Stop the car.'

'What happened?' asked Jack, bewildered.

'Stop it now,' she yelled.

Jack immediately put his foot on the brakes. The vehicle came to a screeching halt on the side of the highway. Nisha got out and ran to the back of the car, calling out to Jack to open the boot.

Jack complied and got out to join her. Nisha had already opened the briefcase that had been handed to her and was staring at the bundles of notes in it.

'What the hell!' said Jack, when he saw the stacks of cash.

Nisha didn't reply. She searched and found the gunny bag, pulled it open and overturned it. The contents fell out. She recognised Kumar Saurabh's wallet and his favourite pen.

Tears started rolling down her cheeks.

'You can't do this to me,' she yelled, as she began to frantically dial his phone number.

The phone rang continuously, but there was no answer.

Jack took the letter from her hand and read it to make sense of what was happening. Nisha was sobbing and he put his arms around her to hug her. She pushed him away and redialled the number. There was no response.

AN UNEASY ESCAPE

'What should we do with them?'

'We allow them to go. Return their phones and other belongings.'

'Walk away after what they did! I don't understand the games you people play.'

'Do as I say. We want to downplay this entire episode. Pretend that it never happened.'

'But they made recordings. They saw it with their own eyes.'

'All the recordings have been destroyed. They have no evidence, except for their personal statements. I have built an alibi for Pankaj Adhikari. He was never here. It will be their word against ours.'

Anton walked over to the interrogation room where the three were being held and looked in through the peephole. Jill and the photographer looked worried, but Karishma was calm and composed. She had a certain poise that would have been wonderful to break.

Anton grinned. He knew how lucky she had been. Her confidence was completely misplaced and was going to get her killed someday. The only reason she was walking out alive was because she had failed to corner Pankaj Adhikari, providing him with a way out to escape her onslaught. Had she succeeded in her act and not left him with any choice, then she would have ended at the bottom of the river. He wondered if she would look so confident if knew how close she had come to her death.

Anton opened the door and walked into the room startling them. 'Here you go,' he said, handing them their personal belongings. 'You are all free to leave.'

Jill exchanged glances with the other two, surprised that they were being let off so easily. It was too good to be true. 'You must be one hell of a big shot, dear,' she said, to Karishma. 'No one gets out of the lower deck with a kiss on their cheek.'

'Better sense seems to have prevailed on them,' replied Karishma, as she fiddled through her phone. 'Ha-ha! Just as I expected. All data has been erased.'

'The storage of my camera has also been cleaned,' said the photographer.

'Ha-ha! All evidence gone. We are as good as our word.'

'Someone seems to have gone through a lot of effort cleaning the data on my phone?' said Karishma, staring at Anton.

'I don't know what you are talking about,' said Anton, feigning ignorance. 'Now, if you don't mind, I have other work to do. One of my men will guide you out of the casino.'

A few minutes later, they walked out, escorted by a few men from security. Anton ensured that every camera in the casino recorded their exit. This was the way Bobby wanted it.

Once they had reached the jetty, the security staff returned to the ship.

'Do we have a case?' asked Jill.

'The photographs were the scoop. There is no story without them. It is our word against theirs.'

'Shit! I got carried away. We should have made a faster exit.'

'I don't think we would have gotten out. But we should have sent off the pics immediately.'

'The thought never occurred to me.'

'It did to me, I even tried sending one of them on WhatsApp. But the signal was too damn weak for it go.'

'Anyway, you will get that parcel soon. Work on it, and let me know if you need anything else. And take care, will you? I don't know why they let us go, but it is making me very uneasy.'

'I will do that,' replied Karishma, handing her visiting card to Jill. 'If these people bug you, call me on this number.'

They said goodbye and went their separate ways.

Jill's home was an hour's drive from the jetty at Panaji. She was jittery all the way. She kept wondering why they had been let off so easily. *What game was Pankaj Adhikari playing?*

It was only after she entered her home and locked the front door that she finally felt a little at ease. But, it was a false sense of security. She didn't notice the two men sitting comfortably on her sofa in the dark. As she turned around to switch on the lights, one of them silently rose up and pushed her forward towards the coffee table. Her legs crashed into it and she fell hard. Her head crashed against the ground and her phone went flying.

She cried out in excruciating pain as a man sat on her back, pinning her to the ground while pulling her hair backwards. As her mouth gasped in pain, he put a piece of cloth inside it to gag her. He continued to apply pressure on her head and pull her hair backwards.

Despite the excruciating pain, she could feel someone ripping her skirt apart and pulling on her underwear. She tried to fight back and keep her legs together but she was no match for the brute strength. Jill moved in and out of consciousness. Then the man sitting on top of her pulled out a syringe containing heroin and gave her a shot in her arm. After a few minutes, she overdosed. The second man continued to torment her as froth filled her mouth choking her.

Jill disappeared that night. No one saw her again.

PART 3

FLYING INTO THE RISING SUN

The conversation between them continued late into the night. Jesse lost count of how many joints he rolled. He became so engrossed in the conversation that he forgot to keep watch for Baldy to come off a motor boat on to the jetty. He had no clue that Baldy was, at that moment, coming in and out of consciousness.

It was only when the birds began to chirp outside that Kumar Saurabh emerged from his trance. They had been sitting inside the car for some hours smoking weed. Dawn was breaking.

'I better leave now, my friend.'

'Why? We were warming up.'

'I need to be somewhere. I have some unfinished business.'

'You want me to drop you.'

'Oh no! This is a journey that I must make myself.'

'Aren't you forgetting something?' said Jesse, as he opened the glove compartment of the Mercedes and pulled out a small pouch of the white powder.

Kumar Saurabh's eyes lit up as he put his hand in his back pocket to pull out his wallet.

'Fuck! I can't believe this,' he swore.

'What happened?' asked Jesse.

'I left my wallet at the casino. I don't have money to pay you.'

'You can always pay later,' said Jesse.

'No, my friend. This is a burden that I don't wish to carry.'

'Then take it,' said Jesse. 'It is a gift, not a loan.'

Kumar Saurabh got out of the vehicle and strolled towards his Ferrari. As soon as he reached the parked vehicle, he pulled out the pouch from his pocket and pored its contents on the bonnet of his car.

Since he did not have his wallet, which contained his credit cards and currency, he used his pocket comb to crush the white powder into fine particles, before forming two thick lines. He pulled out the pollution certificate from the glove compartment, rolled it up and snorted the two lines of cocaine in quick succession. Then he looked up at the sky one last time—the moon was setting and the stars were fading. The chirping of the birds had become louder. It was time to go.

He settled in the bucket seat and turned on the ignition of the 3 litre, twelve-cylinder engine. The beast growled, waiting to be unleashed. He blasted the music, and pulled the gear across and back into first.

Keep your eyes on the road … Your hands upon the wheel, the music blared in the background.

The cocaine had found its way around the mucus membrane and was getting absorbed into his blood vessels. Once absorbed, it flowed along the blood stream to the rest of his body, arriving at the blood brain barrier i.e., the entry gate to the brain.

He stamped on the gas and put the beast into second gear. His body pressed back into the bucket seat by the sheer acceleration of the vehicle, his hair flowed against the wind.

Let it roll, baby, roll…
Let it roll, baby, roll … Let it roll, all night long.

As the cocaine made its way past the blood brain barrier, it stimulated the neurotransmitters in the brain, specifically dopamine—the natural happy drug. Kumar Saurabh had started to trip.

You gotta roll, roll, roll … You gotta thrill my soul, alright.

Under normal circumstances, the amount of dopamine should have returned to its original levels shortly after being released. But the cocaine prevented it from recycling, ensuring excessive amounts of dopamine in his body cells. Kumar Saurabh was now on a euphoric high, feeling invincible.

Somewhere in the background his phone rang continuously. But the music was loud and he was too tripped out to give a shit. Had he bothered to see, he would have found his daughter on the phone, calling him in desperation, hoping that he would stop his madness.

He stepped harder on the pedal, putting the beast into a third, and then a fourth in quick succession. As a deadly concoction of fuel and air gushed into the V12, the engine screamed in all its fury, hitting the 7000-rpm mark to create such a mesmerising earth-shattering noise that would have given the Sydney Orchestra a run for its money. Soon, the imagery on either side of the road became hazy, as the beast roared at 130 miles an hour.

The future's uncertain … And the end is always near.

Dawn was breaking, the horizon filled with colours of red and yellow as the Ferrari raced towards the expressway leading to the airport on the outskirts of Panaji. As the vehicle approached the bridge on top of the Mandovi, the first rays of the rising sun hit Kumar Saurabh's eyes. He smiled and stepped on the gas, deliberately steering the beast towards the right to hit the elevated pathway at 130 miles an hour. Things happened very fast thereafter as the vehicle took off into the air like a bird which had been uncaged, flying across the rising sun and diving into the embrace of the Mandovi river below.

In those final moments, before the vehicle splashed into the river, Kumar Saurabh's life flashed before his eyes. The mirror of his alter ego was finally shattered. He didn't see any fame, glory or fans. He didn't even see the night when his first movie became a blockbuster hit. Instead, he saw an image of his doting mother, the love in her eyes for her son. He saw the expression of awe on his face when he had first met his bride to be. He saw the pride and happiness when their child was born. He saw Nisha, he saw her smile, and he heard her forgiveness.

As the Ferrari crashed into the river, water immediately flooded inside it. Kumar Saurabh made no attempt to release the seat belt. He went down smiling with the love of his life to the bottom of the river.

Death wasn't quick, but it was certainly king-size.

It was half past noon when Karishma was woken up out of deep slumber by her phone ringing. She looked at it sleepily, her eyes only half open, trying to make up her mind whether to accept the call or not. It was her editor. She didn't have a choice.

'Hello,' she said, groggily.

'You still napping?' asked her editor.

'Yeah, we had an adventurous night. Got very late,' she replied.

'So, I guess you haven't seen the news?'

'Why? What happened?'

'Kumar Saurabh, the actor, is dead.'

'What? I saw him last night at the casino. How? What happened?'

'Looks like an accident. They found his Ferrari in the Mandovi.'

'I don't know what to say. I got his autograph last evening on a piece of tissue paper. Hold on, will you.'

She got up from bed and ran towards her jeans which were hung behind the door. She searched the pockets and found the tissue paper. It was there, the last autograph Kumar Saurabh had given. She came back to her bed and picked up the phone. 'This is so surreal.'

'We need a story in the evening paper. Do you want to take the lead? You can add a personal touch since you were perhaps the last journalist to have met him.'

'Sure! I will get dressed and come to office.'

Karishma put down the phone and stretched her body. She took a quick shower and dressed. Her mind was full of the events at the casino. *I must check up on Jill sometime during the day*, she thought. *I hope they are not pestering her.*

An hour later, she was at the office, having an animated discussion with her editor about the events of the previous evening.

'I want to write this story,' she said.

'Without the photographs, you have nothing.'

'What do you mean nothing? I am an eye witness and so is Jill.'

'It is your word against theirs. For all you know, they will have built an alibi by now. Don't you know how these things work?'

'You want me to drop this story?'

'Not at all, darling. I want you to take a tactical step backwards. Give them the impression that you are no longer pursuing the story. Let them breathe and relax, as you work under radar on the real story. By the way, has that package arrived?'

'Not yet, but she said it should be on its way. Let me call her in any case.'

'Sure! Do that and keep me informed.'

Karishma walked out of the editor's room and went to her desk. She dialled Jill. All she got was a pre-recorded message that said, 'the phone is out of coverage area.'

Hmm! Interesting. This one's a pro. Already gone underground.

She went to the police station to get their version of events on the death of Kumar Saurabh. On the way, she dialled Jill a few more times but got the same message every time.

It's nothing, she told herself. There was no cause for worry. But she felt uneasy. Something didn't seem right. She remembered Jill's expression of surprise and fear when they let them off without any harm. Had they done something to her? She kept trying to push that frightening thought out of her mind without much success.

♦

WAS HE MISSING THE LARGER PICTURE?

Anton was eating lunch, but his mind was preoccupied. He had been calling up the Escort Service office since 10 am to talk to Ruby. He was keen to know what had happened between her and Balwant. It was a well-known fact that ladyboys often got away with it. Their customers were too drunk and busy playing with their tits to figure out that what was on offer wasn't what they had paid for. Ruby was smart and Balwant, well, to put it mildly, not the smartest. At least, that's what Anton thought.

Lucky bitch. I can't believe that the drunk is still romping her. If he had caught on to the act, she would have been back within hours.

He glanced at his watch again. It showed half past two.

What the fuck! There's no reason why I can't call Ruby at this time.

He picked up his phone and dialled. Her phone was switched off. He hesitated for minute and then dialled Balwant. The phone rang a few times before Balwant answered.

'Hi, Balwant. This is Anton,' he said. 'Enquiring if you had a pleasant evening?' he asked.

'Bastard! You know very well I didn't,' yelled Balwant.

'I am sorry, Balwant, but I don't understand,' said Anton, pretending ignorance.

'Stop wasting my time and ask him or her, or whatever she is.'

'I am sorry. Do you mean that Ruby is not with you?'

'No. I threw her out of my penthouse within minutes of reaching the hotel. I don't know where she is.'

'Oh!'

Before he could say anything else, the phone went dead. Anton laughed out loud, imagining the scene between Ruby and Balwant. 'Where is that bitch?' he wondered aloud. Then he remembered his parting words to her—'I will have you raped every night.' *Must have run away.*

Anton was still fretting over having to let Jack go without getting to punch him at least once, but this news about Ruby cheered him up.

In the evening, he ran into Bobby, who had been busy in meetings all day trying to understand the operations of the casino. 'You woke up on the right side of the bed,' said Bobby, noting Anton's happy face.

'She got caught, Boss,' replied Anton, laughing. 'The fairy tale is over. Balwant threw her out of the room last night.'

'She told you?' asked Bobby, looking a little surprized.

'Balwant did,' replied Anton. 'Ruby seems to have run away.'

'You mean she hasn't returned? Why do you think she has run away?'

'An informed guess? Her fairy tale love affair is over. She had her passport for the first time last evening after more than two years. Also, I had a showdown with her on the casino floor. I might have scared her off.'

'Anton, are you sure that she is gone?'

'Boss, don't worry. There are any number of girls who can replace her.'

'It isn't that. With Ruby gone, every one of Jayesh's closest people has left, except for you. I hope this is a mere coincidence and not something else. I have learned one thing from boss, and that is that there are no coincidences. This makes me jittery.'

'What do you mean?' said Anton. 'Jack left because I caught him cheating and locked him up. Ruby left for reasons that I mentioned. And Jayesh left because you beat him at his own game. I don't see any pattern here, except for the fact that we kicked their ass.'

'Yeah, you are right. Maybe, I am tired and overthinking.'

Bobby walked away, but he wasn't convinced. Instinct told him that all was not well. He left the casino in the evening and decided to drive by Jayesh's house. The house was shut and the lights turned off. Jayesh had left the city. He then called on Nisha and Jack. But they weren't there either. If Anton was correct, then even Ruby had disappeared.

Leaving the casino was one thing. But, why had all of them left the city in such a hurry? Was this also a coincidence? Or was he missing something? Only time would tell.

Nisha and Jack arrived at Bangalore airport a few hours before their flight to Singapore. Jack had driven all the way without a break, except for the mandatory washroom stops. In the beginning, Nisha had tried, without success, to reach her father several times. A few hours into their journey, her worst fears came true with the news on social media of Kumar Saurabh's death. Jack stopped the car on the side of the expressway and tried to console Nisha, but soon realised that it was better for him to let her be, to allow her to deal with her grief. So, they didn't speak much for the rest of the journey.

Nisha kept fiddling with the letter, opening it and reading a few lines and then sinking into a reverie. The letter didn't say much except how grateful Kumar Saurabh was for being forgiven by her. It was a burden that he had carried for long in his heart. Then it went on to add that he had left a small contribution to help with the new life that she was going to start in Singapore.

Nisha wasn't very close to her father, but the fact that he had ended his life in this way disturbed her. She wondered if things would have been different had she been by his side at this time. She went over and over the conversation she had with him at the coffee shop in her mind. He had come to her for reconciliation and she had thrown his past deeds at him, reminding him of the father that he hadn't been. She shouldn't have met him, if all she wanted to do was vent her anger at him. Despite her unforgivably rude behaviour, all he had thought about was how to help her in his final hour. In hindsight, the only consolation was that she had forgiven him. Thank God she had followed Jack's advice. Otherwise, she would have had to live with this burden for the rest of her life.

By the time they crossed immigration, Nisha had come to terms with her father's death. Somewhere in her heart, she knew that this is what he had wanted. He wouldn't have had it any other way. Things would have been no different, even if she had been by his side.

She finally put a hand on Jack's shoulder and pulled him towards her. They stood there hugging each other for a while. Then, she walked over to the WH Smith counter and looked at the stack of evening papers. Finally, there was a smile on her face.

What Kumar Saurabh had failed to achieve in the latter part of his life, he had managed with his death. He had made front page news in every newspaper and tabloid across the country. They carried his photograph along with that of his Ferrari, the love of his life. This was the way he would have wanted it. It was the only way to die.

IT IS BEAUTIFUL!

Ruby arrived in Phuket the next evening, around the same time that Jack and Nisha were boarding their flight to Singapore. She took a connecting flight to Chiang Mai and made her way to her village at the outskirts of the city. In Thai culture, daughters were expected to take care of their mother in her old age. Even though Ruby was born a male child, she had always played the role of a daughter and it was only fair that she shared some of her new found wealth with her mother. Life in the village had changed very little since her last visit. But, unlike the last time, most of her friends no longer lived there. They had left for the cities in search of a livelihood.

Ruby spent the next few days in the village reliving her childhood. She helped her mother cook some basic food in the morning before setting out to herd the buffalos to the field. Then they rested under a tree, eating their packed lunch and gossiping about the time gone by. Ruby's mother was very intrigued about her adventures in India. Ruby told her about the fast-paced life in a casino. She also confided to her about Balwant.

After spending a few days with her mother, Ruby went to meet her elder sister. She didn't have any biological sisters, but she called the *kathoey*, who had helped her transition from a confused soul trapped in the wrong body to her new identity, her sister. She worked in the entertainment industry. She had aged significantly in the past 3 years since Ruby had last met her. A hard life and constant abuse had taken its toll on her sister's body. Ruby hugged her and felt very sad at her condition. She realised how fortunate she had been, thanks to Jayesh. They sat and chatted like long lost friends. Ruby tried to give her some money, but she refused to accept it. So she woke up early at dawn the next day and left a bundle of 100-dollar notes under her pillow and left without saying goodbye.

Ruby went to Bangkok and admitted herself into a hospital which specialised in gender reassignment surgeries, also known as sex change operations. She had been taking female hormones for a long time and had already gone under the knife a few times to make her facial appearance more feminine. Gender reassignment was the final step in her journey to becoming a woman.

Despite much progress in the field of medicine, every medical procedure involved a certain degree of risk. Doctors explained to Ruby how the surgery would be done and the risks associated with it. It would involve removing her male genitalia. This would be followed by a vaginoplasty, the creation of a vagina. Upon hearing the procedure, Ruby was suddenly lost in deep thought. All these years she had lived her life in a state of confusion, her mind in constant disagreement with her body. Come tomorrow, once and for all she would remove this dichotomy. She heard the faint voice of the doctor in the background, 'after the procedure, you can enjoy orgasms like any other woman.' The entire process would take only two weeks. Ruby excitedly agreed to the procedure and signed on the dotted line.

Later that night, she took out the mobile phone that Balwant had given her and put it on charge. Then she went to sleep. Tomorrow would be a new beginning.

The surgery was performed at dawn under general anaesthesia. She woke up the after almost 24 hours. She felt different. She excitedly pulled up her sheet to see the transformation, but it was still covered in plaster. She would have to wait for a few days until the plaster was removed.

The next few days were very troublesome. She tried to watch television to pass the time, but she was very restless. She looked at the mobile phone more than once to make sure that it wasn't on silent, that it had a strong signal. Almost two weeks were coming to an end and she wondered why Balwant had not yet called her. To add to her anxiety, she still had not been able to see her transformation.

Finally, on the fifteenth day, the mobile rang. She took the call on the first ring. Balwant's reassuring voice came down the line and she closed her eyes in relief and joy. 'How are you darling?' he said. 'Did you miss me?'

'I missed you tons,' she replied with a smile.

'Where are you? Have you done what you had set out to do?'

'I am in Bangkok. Still recovering. I should be out in a few days.'

'Great! I am in Phuket. Will share my contact. Hope to see you soon.'

The line was cut.

'Who was that?' asked the nurse, who had been tending to her for the past week.

'He is part of the reason for me to have done this,' she replied.

'Oh darling! He better be worth it.'

'He is worth every bit,' she replied. 'And much more. How much longer?' she asked, indicating the plaster.

'If you are lucky, maybe tomorrow or the day after.'

She gave a sigh of relief.

'I had somehow held myself together all these days. But now that he is here, I can't wait to be with him.'

'Patience, darling,' said the nurse. 'Let me speak with the doctor. Let's see what he has to say.'

She lay there flipping channels on the television set, but she was thinking of Balwant. There were so many questions that she wanted to ask him. She still hadn't understood what he had done or how, except that he hadn't lost money as it appeared. That was the most important thing for her.

'I believe that there is someone special that you had rather be with,' said the doctor when he came to see her with the nurse.

Ruby smiled.

'How are you feeling?' he asked.

'I am feeling fine, doctor,' she replied. 'Do you think that we can cut this plaster?' she asked.

'Let me see,' he replied, as he used one of the instruments to have a better look at the stitches.

'Hmm! It isn't completely dry yet. But we can let you go on the promise that this will remain out of bounds for at least the next week.'

'Don't worry, doctor. I won't let anyone come near it,' replied Ruby with a wide grin.

'Ok, in that case, let's proceed with it,' he replied.

Ruby was moved to a well-lit room with a large full-length mirror. She sat down on a specialised wheel chair.

'I am now going to cut the plaster,' said the doctor. 'Thereafter, we are going to spread your legs. Let me know if you feel any pain.'

Ruby nodded. She could hear the plaster being cut. Her heart was pumping loudly now. She was sure that the doctor could hear her heart beat.

'Calm down, dear,' he said, putting a hand on her shoulder. 'It is going to be fine.'

But the anxiety was killing her.

The plaster suddenly fell to the ground with a soft thud. She felt a sense of freedom between her legs.

The nurse held on to both her legs and slowly began to spread them wide apart. She stopped midway.

'Any pain,' she asked.

'No,' replied Ruby, her mind somewhere else.

She spread them wider.

'Still no pain?' asked the doctor.

'No,' replied Ruby.

'Ok. In that case, we will leave you now to see it for yourself,' said the doctor.

As soon as the doctor and the nurse left the room, Ruby turned around the wheelchair to face the large mirror.

As she saw the first glimpse of the transformation, tears filled her eyes.

'It's beautiful,' she whispered.

EASIER SAID THAN DONE

Investigation into Kumar Saurabh's death kept Karishma busy for a few days. She had written a small story for the evening edition, but a well-researched follow-up appeared a few days later. It was clear to her within hours that this wasn't a case of a random accident, as it had first seemed, but that of a pre-meditated suicide. Kumar Saurabh had been found sitting in the bucket seat with his seat belt fastened. There were no signs of struggle. People taking an early morning walk had seen the car flying into the river. They had corroborated the evidence that while the car was being driven fast, it was not out of control. There were no skid marks on the road. None of the passerby remembered hearing a vehicle skidding out of control. Karishma replayed her meeting with Kumar Saurabh several times in her mind. It disturbed her that she hadn't picked up any signs of an impending suicide. There was nothing in his behaviour to suggest that he was going to end his life. He had met her and the others with the same charm and warmth reserved for fans. This was undoubtedly the best performance of his life.

But, once the story ended, thoughts about Jill's disappearance completely consumed her. Jill was still unreachable. Even if she had gone into hiding, she would definitely have made contact with her to tell her that all was well. The fact that four days had now passed without a word from her meant that something was wrong. Karishma was very anxious.

On the morning of the fifth day, she begged her editor to pull strings and help her locate Jill. They made a few calls and were able to pull out Jill's address from the records of the telephone company. Karishma immediately went to her house, only to find it locked.

She returned to the office tired and dejected. But, the sight of a package lying on her desk got her adrenaline flowing. She opened it like a child opens a gift box, ripping the outer packing to get to its contents.

The first thing she pulled out was a signed letter handwritten by Jill, listing the contents of the package. The last two lines read that under no circumstances was Karishma to drop the story. It had to be pursued at all costs, even if it meant that she risked putting Jill's life in danger. The letter further strengthened Karishma's resolve. She went through the other contents of the package. She scanned the documents for both relevance and completeness. She wanted to make sure that everything that Jill had confessed to her earlier was backed by relevant documents.

All this while, her editor's advice boomed in her ears: 'Make sure that every assertion and conjecture is borne out by facts. You are emotionally connected to this story and I don't want your personal biases to influence it.'

Finally, after spending an hour examining the contents of the package, Karishma took a deep breath. It was all there. There was more than she had expected to find. She had her work cut out for the next week. She was going against the rich and mighty, exposing the underbelly of the state. 'I am going to nail these bastards,' she said.

But there was one thing left to do before she went to work. The next day in the morning, she went to the police station to file a missing person's report. It was easier said than done. The cops asked her many questions about her relationship with Jill. They figured out that Karishma had only recently met Jill and didn't know her well enough. How could she be certain that Jill had gone missing? What if it was a simple case of a person travelling? The phone was switched off because she didn't wish to be disturbed. Karishma knew that if she wanted, she could have made her arguments convincing and forced the cops to register a report. But, to do so, she would have had to share information about the happenings at the casino. She didn't want to link Jill's disappearance with Pankaj Adhikari. It would have immediately raised eyebrows. Her editor had warned her not to divulge too much information because it could reach Pankaj Adhikari's ears and jeopardise the publication of her story. This is what Jill wanted more than anything else.

Eventually, she walked out of the police station without getting a report registered. The only way forward was to put in all her effort and get that story published. Once the story was out, the police would be forced to file that report.

DON'T RETURN EMPTY-HANDED

A fortnight had passed since Bobby had taken over as the CEO of the casino. He was happy. He was a hands-on person and had spent most of his time in understanding the operations of the casino. In particular, he focused on activities that happened behind the scenes to run such an establishment. He made some changes in the reporting structure, firing or reassigning employees either disliked by him, or not aligned to his way of thinking. Everything seemed to be proceeding smoothly. He couldn't have imagined a smoother transition, given that he had taken over quite abruptly from Jayesh, without any period of overlap.

Now that he had a good hold on operations, he moved his attention to the front end. Jayesh was a natural when it came to socialising with customers. He was warm, flamboyant and a great talker. Bobby, on the other hand, was awkward in social situations. He wasn't much of talker and struggled to make conversation with customers. He made up for this by throwing freebies and perquisites at the high-rollers. In a materialistic world, freebies mattered and the high-rollers seemed to love him, at least on the outside.

Even though he was busy, Bobby had kept a close eye on the investigation into the fraud. He sensed that there was more dirt than met the eye. He was frustrated with the slow pace of the investigations. 'You have made no progress,' he told Anton. 'Nothing new has emerged in the past fortnight which wasn't already known.'

'These things take time, boss,' replied Anton.

Anton kept going round and round in circles. His investigation always pointed towards Louis, who had already confessed, and Jack, who was no longer there to defend himself.

'Has it occurred to you, that Jayesh might have set us on a wild goose chase?' he said to Bobby. 'A parting gift as he left. He is drinking Piña Coladas on some secluded beach as we go round in circles trying to find what doesn't exist.'

Putting the blame on Jack and Louis was the most convenient thing to do, but Bobby wasn't buying it. Not yet, at least. 'You could be right, Anton. Maybe, he has made a fool of us. But I want you to arrive at that conclusion after you have investigated the matter and not before.'

'There is nothing further to investigate. All evidence implicates two people, both of whom we had in our custody, until you let one of them walk away.'

Bobby realised that Anton wasn't going to give in so easily. So, he suggested the unthinkable. It wasn't a serious suggestion, but one made to push Anton. 'I was thinking, we should hand over the investigation to the cops,' he said. 'We need a new line of thinking.'

Anton was horrified. 'You can't be serious, boss! We have never involved cops in our business. They are on our payroll, so that they don't put their nose in our business,' he said quickly, nervously.

'I know, but if you don't give me some leads soon, I will have no choice. If it's not the cops, then I will have to get personally involved. I am going to rip every assumption and start afresh.'

'But there is nothing to find,' replied Anton, a little agitated now. He didn't understand why his words were falling on deaf ears. He had gotten away with a lot worse in the past. Why was Bobby not letting him be?

'Go and tell that to the big boss, because I won't,' said Bobby. 'And before you do that, let me tell you one more thing: he believes that there is more to the story.'

For the first time, Anton was afraid. He wasn't scared of anyone, except death. But he realised that it wasn't Bobby who was being unreasonable. The pressure was coming from the top. This would not go away so easily. It was time to find someone else, someone in his own team to take the blame. Anything to get them off his back.

He wondered for the first time whether he had done the right thing by catching them in the act. He was so eager to nail Jack and get his revenge on Baldy that he might have overlooked the risks. Now, if he didn't play it well, it would come to bite him in the ass.

Bobby was pleased that his frank chat with Anton bore results. Anton had finally opened up to the idea that there could be more people involved in the fraud. There was nothing that the right amount of pressure couldn't achieve. People needed different triggers to get the best out of them. For Anton, the only trigger was fear. Otherwise, he was a bully who would keep stepping on your toes, and if you didn't push back, then soon he would be stomping on your nose.

Anton had found a way to ward off the pressure. He had identified two people, one in his own team and the other in Jack's team, who would take the fall, if it came to that. One of them had delivered the envelope that fateful day containing the instructions, which Anton now denied. The other one had been seen fiddling in Jack's room that evening.

Just as Anton thought he had things in hand at last, Bobby called him one evening for a meeting. He had been recently informed by the credit department that Balwant and his troupe of villagers had not yet paid up. It was nothing unusual, given their past payment history. They always paid. But, for the first time, this credit was outstanding on his watch, and Bobby wanted to be very sure that there was no problem. He still had that bad feeling in his gut that something was wrong. But he didn't wish to share his feelings with Anton. He had figured Anton out. Anton had his limitations. He was a great soldier, but not a General. The problem was that he often thought of himself as a General.

'There is an outstanding against Balwant,' he said. 'I want you to look into it.'

'Nothing to worry about,' replied Anton. 'He always pays up. Sometimes after a week, sometimes two.'

'I know. I still want you to look into it.'

'Ok, Boss. I will give him a call if you are losing your sleep over it.'

'I am not, but I want to be sure.

Anton called up Balwant later that evening, but his phone was out of reach. He tried one more time before going to bed. There was no response. The next morning, as soon as he woke up, he tried reaching him again, but couldn't. Now, Anton started feeling uneasy. He dressed up and went to office. On his way, he called the office and asked the credit team to be present for a meeting.

As soon as he arrived at the casino, he went to meet them.

'Have you tried to contact Balwant?' he asked.

'Yes, sir,' came the reply. 'But he is not reachable.'

'For how long?'

'We have been trying for the past three days.'

Anton was jittery, but tried to underplay the situation. 'He could be traveling, or lying drunk somewhere. Have you tried contacting any of the others from his group?'

'Sir, we tried contacting them yesterday. But they were also unreachable.'

Now Anton was afraid and angry. He lunged at one of them and pulled him up by his collar. 'What the fuck!' he yelled. 'When were you planning to tell me, you piece of shit? Is Bobby aware?'

'No, sir,' came the reply in a whisper.

Anton let the collar go and rushed to meet Bobby. On the way, he called up some of his men and told them to prepare for emergency travel.

'Boss, there is a problem,' said Anton. 'Neither Balwant nor any other member of his troupe is contactable. I am immediately flying to Delhi with a few men.'

Bobby wasn't surprised. He let out a loud laugh. The kind of laugh that made even Anton worry. 'I knew it,' he said. 'I knew that something was wrong when Jayesh and his team disappeared overnight. But you downplayed my doubts. Now go and find them. For your own sake, I hope that you don't return empty handed.'

LET US SHOW THEM HOW IT IS DONE

There was an unusually long queue in front of the Hainanese Chicken Rice stall at the Maxwell Hawker Centre in Singapore. There was always a queue at dinner time, but never as long as this.

Nisha was taking orders at the stall. She was still getting used to the Singaporean accent and learning a few words of Singlish in the process. Jack had to deliver on the orders. He was finding it hard to keep pace with the flow of orders and were it not for the patience of the crowd, they would have been in trouble.

Mr & Mrs Tan sat a few tables away from the stall, Mr Tan enjoying a chilled bottle of Tsing Tao beer and Mrs Tan sipping on some refreshing Calamansi juice.

'Shouldn't we help him?' she asked, overflowing with motherly love. 'He is clearly struggling.'

Mr Tan took a few sips of the beer straight from the bottle. He was rather enjoying the sight of his son in a bit of nervous sweat, trying to keep pace with the growing queue of hungry customers. Even the seasoned Mr Tan struggled at times to keep pace with the crowds during dinner hour. So, he was not really bothered.

'No need,' he replied. 'He can fend for himself. He was pestering me for the past week to let him work at the shop.'

'I know,' said Mrs Tan. 'But I don't think he had a clue how much work it involves.'

'I know,' grinned Mr Tan. 'He thought it was going to be a walk in the Botanical Gardens. "'Papa, let me ease your burden for a day,'" mimicked Mr Tan sarcastically. 'Now, let him fulfil his wish.'

There was silence.

'Actually, I think I will ask him to work for another week. What do you think, Mrs Tan? We both can do with some rest,' said Mr Tan with a playful smile.

'No way,' she said sternly. 'You will do no such thing. At least, think about the poor girl. What will she think of us?'

'Hmm!' Mr Tan gave her a pensive look. 'Perhaps, I should spend the next week bonding with her, while you and your son work at the shop.'

'I am fine with that,' replied Mrs Tan. 'But, don't you complain after a week.'

'Why should I complain?'

'I notice that Jack has been handing them larger portions of the chicken than you do. A day wouldn't make a difference. But if he were to continue doing so for a week, customers will expect the same from you.'

'What?' exclaimed Mr Tan, the playful look wiped off his face. 'I gave your boy one measly job, and even that he can't do well. I will tell him in the evening how much money he has lost for me today.'

Mrs Tan laughed. 'So, I guess the two of us will be working at the counter tomorrow?'

Mr Tan was quiet and Mrs Tan had a good laugh. After a while, she said, 'I like Nisha. The poor girl has been through difficult times.'

'She is a smart girl. I like her too. For once, our boy has done well.'

'But sometimes I worry,' said Mrs Tan.

'Why?'

'She comes from a broken family.'

'You disappoint me, Mrs Tan. You must evaluate the girl for her qualities, not her parents. She didn't choose them.'

'But she has a choice now.'

'Exactly! I see her making every attempt to settle down. A new country, a new family, it must be difficult. And yet, the girl is always smiling. She is always trying.'

Mrs Tan smiled.

'I am so glad to hear that. I was only testing you, Mr Tan. I have already accepted her as my daughter.'

'Oh! So, how did I do, Mrs Tan?'

'You came through with flying colours.'

'Then I guess it calls for a celebration, Mrs Tan. Why don't you get me another bottle of beer?'

Mrs Tan went to buy a bottle of beer and returned after a few minutes to an empty table. She didn't have to look around for her husband. She simply walked to the Chicken Rice counter where the father and son were working hand in hand, as Nisha took in the orders. It was one happy family.

When Mr Tan saw her at the counter, he said, 'Mrs Tan, let us show the children how it is done.'

'What about the beer?' she asked.

'Oh! That was never for me. It was for them.'

HE HAD PLAYED THEM ALL

As soon as Anton left for the airport, Bobby went to the surveillance unit office to examine old records and files. He wanted to understand the case first hand so that he could not only cover his own ass, but find an escape goat to take the fall as well. Pankaj Adhikari wasn't going to take the loss of a few million dollars lightly. Imagine, someone actually stealing from a politician! It wasn't about the money alone, but also about reputation. If word got out about the fraud, he would become the laughing stock in his circle.

Bobby suspected that there was a link between Jayesh and Balwant. There were too many coincidences for his comfort. He wanted to understand how Balwant had escaped attention for so long. Every time a person won or lost significant sums of money at a casino; he came under the eye of the online surveillance unit. It was said that it was easy to beat the house at a casino, but to remain undetected was almost impossible. How was it then that Balwant had remained below the radar and undetected for so long? Or, was it that he had been identified, but let go by an insider? Was there any evidence to suggest that Jayesh had been too considerate towards him?

The records showed that on several occasions, the surveillance unit was interested in Balwant. Not because he won large sums, but because he lost too often. But, each time Anton had laughed off the suggestion that there was something fishy, or untoward that required further investigations. 'The fucking drunk hangs out with Ruby. What can you expect?' His deep dislike of Ruby had blinded him.

The superstition about Ruby, that anybody in her company was bound to lose, had been nurtured and surreptitiously made known to all the regulars. Anton firmly believed it and had done his bit to spread it around just to make things difficult for Ruby. Despite that, Balwant always asked for her. This should have raised eyebrows, but because he kept losing and not winning, no one looked closely at what was going on. There was nothing on record to suggest that Jayesh had favoured him. In fact, it was Anton who had pushed her to be with him, despite her own reservations.

Bobby asked them to pull out the recordings of the dates when Balwant lost large sums of money. He saw the tapes many times over. Initially, he didn't see any trend emerge, but soon he noticed that the same set of people were appearing at the table. They were not there every time, so it was not too obvious; but every now and then they moved to the table on which Balwant was playing. Bobby started concentrating on some of these faces and found that they won on the bets that Balwant played. But, none of these faces had ever evoked any interest because their winnings were too small compared to the large bets that Balwant took. Everyone was busy counting the money that Balwant lost and missed the smaller sums that were won by a group of six or seven counter bets. The number of these smaller bets were so large, they often ran into double digits.

Bobby began to go back in time to figure out how long this racket had been running. After a few hours of work, he traced it back to almost the time when Balwant first appeared at the casino. Balwant wasn't the dumbass he pretended to be. The son of a bitch was running an offset betting scandal, where he lost money only to be won by others of his own group. Over a period of time, he and his troupe of villagers successfully raised their credit scores with the casino. Most of them had started with zero credit and moved up to a hundred thousand dollars. As for Balwant, the amount was much larger and ran into millions of dollars.

It was no coincidence that all this culminated on the night of the big inauguration. Balwant asked for the largest amount of credit and it was disbursed by none other than Bobby himself, with a lot of aggressive cajoling from Anton. Jayesh had played this entire piece smartly, not even coming into the picture. Had he intervened, maybe Bobby would have sensed trouble and declined the request. Bobby waited for Anton to return, but he already knew that he would come back empty handed. The big question that needed answering was whether Anton was an accomplice in this racket, or was he simply at the wrong place at the wrong time.

When Bobby returned to his room that evening, he found a small parcel waiting for him on his desk. In it were a few photographs. There was nothing else, no note or letter explaining what it was.

The photographs had been taken from a distance with a telephoto lens. One of the figures was unmistakably that of Anton. This implied that someone was tailing Anton. He could not decipher the others in the photographs. He examined the photographs closely. One of the figures looked familiar. He picked up the photograph and ran to the lower deck of the ship. Anton had disfigured Baldy's face, but Bobby still had no trouble identifying him.

'Fucking hell, you were all together in this scheme until Anton decided to turn you in,' said Bobby, as he showed the photograph to Baldy. Baldy didn't mutter a word. But Bobby didn't need him to say anything. 'I guess that's the reason the investigation is progressing slowly. Did Anton assure you that he will let you off soon?' But Baldy was in no mood to talk. 'I have special plans for you, buddy,' Bobby said, infuriated with him. 'Your worst nightmares have come true.'

Bobby slowly walked back to his office. He wondered who had sent the photographs. It had to be Jayesh. This meant that he knew on the day of the fraud that Anton was behind it. The son of a bitch had kept quiet about the real culprit. Why?

Bobby smiled grimly. Pankaj Adhikari was right. There could never be so many coincidences on the same night. Jayesh bloody well knew about the occupant of the Presidential Suite. Perhaps, Ruby had said something that gave away the identity of the VIP. It wasn't a sweet victory after all. Jayesh had played them all, handing his head on a platter, knowing very well that Pankaj Adhikari would fire him, thus giving him the exit that he needed so badly.

Why did he need the exit? Obviously, because he knew that Balwant's act was coming to a Grand Finale that evening. Shit would hit the fan in the next few days. He knew that Balwant would abscond with a few million dollars, enough to fund a new life for Jayesh in a city of his choice.

There was only one question which still needed answering. Why did Jayesh decide to share the photographs now? Bobby mulled over it for a while. He was sure that while Anton might have been an accomplice in the fraud involving the black jack dealer, he had no clue about the racket involving Balwant.

Bobby laughed aloud. 'Jayesh, you son of a bitch,' he said in appreciation. 'I will never mess with a poker player again.'

THE HOSTILE VILLAGES

By the time Anton and three men from his team arrived at Delhi, it was already late evening. He was met at the hotel by the head of a recovery team which worked with most of the private banks. Anton didn't know the geography nor the local language and had decided to hire some local muscle men who were better versed with the area.

When Anton gave Balwant's address to the local guys, they looked apprehensive. He took the head of the team to the bar for a few drinks and then casually asked him the reason for their discomfort.

'Nobody lends to them. Banks, NBFCs (Non-banking financial companies), not even the money lenders.'

'Why? Do they have that bad a credit history?'

'No. That is not the reason. But, if they decide not to give you something, then it is next to impossible to take it back from them. It is what we call a negative area. Repossession is next to impossible there.'

'I have heard stories about Land Cruisers in front of every house. If the banks haven't lent them money, then who has?'

'They are all purchased on straight payment in cash. As I said, no one lends to them.'

'What do you suggest we do? I get the impression that you are chickening out.'

'No Sir. I am not chickening out. I am appraising you of the reality. It is important that we understand what we are up against. We will run this operation according to our rules. We will decide when to hit and when to exit. It will be our call about when we need to withdraw. Do you agree?'

Anton didn't agree with any of it, but he nodded.

'Good. We will hit them at dawn tomorrow. Take them by surprise. Before word gets out of our visit, we will be out of the village and on our way back.'

Accordingly, at 4:30 am the next morning, three Mahindra Scorpios filled with a dozen muscle men made their way through the dusty roads of Delhi. Within half an hour they had crossed the border and were now travelling on the Delhi Jaipur National Highway. In another 15 minutes, the SUVs had turned left on to a dusty village road. They drove on it for a good half an hour before reaching their destination. It was 5:45 am. This was the furthest village on their map. They wanted to hit it first and then make their way backwards towards Delhi. The idea was that there should be no road block on the way out.

Three men got out of the SUV and walked towards the house. The rest remained in the car with the engine running. Anton moved towards the back to personally receive the person. He was raring to go and hoped that there would be some opportunity for him to warm his hands.

One of the men knocked on the door. After a few seconds, he knocked again. The door opened and a middle-aged man appeared.

'Kadam Singh?'

The guy nodded, his eyes still not fully open. Before he knew it, two guys picked him up, while the third gagged his mouth. It was all over within 30 seconds and they were driving out of the village. The gagged man struggled in the back seat of the SUV giving Anton the opportunity to give him two quick raps across his face. They drove a few kilometres away from the village before stopping the vehicle a little away from the road to interrogate the guy.

Luckily, this time Anton took out his folder to check the amount of money outstanding against him and happened to glance at the photograph attached. Then he looked carefully at the man in custody. There was some mistake.

'Who is this?' he asked.

'Kadam Singh,' came the reply from one of the guys in the recovery team.

Anton immediately took off the cloth from the gagged man's mouth.

'Are you Kadam Singh?' he asked.

'*Chutiye* (Fucker), why don't you go and ask your mother!' came back the reply. 'You have the wrong man. You better get the fuck out of here before I reach my house.'

Anton looked once again at the photograph. He knew that they had the wrong man. He squeezed the man's mouth with his right hand. As his mouth opened, he put the cloth inside it again to gag him. Then he moved backwards, and with all his fury punched him in the face. The guy passed out.

'Throw him outside and let's go to the next house. This time take the fucking photograph with you before gagging and kidnapping the guy.

It was the same story at the next house. This time they did not bother to pick up the man. It became clear that the fraudsters had used false identities.

'Should we call it off?' asked the team leader of the recovery team.

'Not yet. We will visit one more house. Let us go to Balwant's house. He was undoubtedly their ring leader. I want to be sure before I go back to Goa.'

They reached Balwant's village at 6:45 am. The villagers noticed the three SUVs filled with musclemen going to

Balwant's house. This was strange and word spread quickly through the village that something was happening.

Anton stepped out of the SUV with two other men and went to the house. A crowd had already gathered. Things did not look good.

Anton knocked on the door. An old woman in her mid-sixties with blank eyes opened the door. '*Tai* (Aunty), is Balwant there?' he asked.

She gave him a curious look without saying a word. Presuming that she had not heard him the first time, or heard him but not registered, Anton asked again. '*Tai*, is Balwant there?'

Suddenly, she covered her face with both her hands and rushed inside, tears rolling down her cheeks.

A few seconds later, there was some commotion inside and an angry old man charged out. 'What do you want? Who are you?' he shouted loudly.

The crowd heard his voice and someone yelled, '*Tau* (Uncle), are these people troubling you?'

Anton looked back. The crowd had swelled to at least two dozen people and was growing. Twelve of them could still manage this crowd, but not for long. If he didn't act fast, things could get out of hand.

'*Tau*, I am from the bank,' he said. 'We have an inoperative account in Balwant's name. There is money in the account. We can't close the account without his signature.'

The old man immediately softened. '*Puttar* (Son), Balwant passed away a few years back,' he replied.

Anton was shocked.

'I see that you weren't aware,' the old man continued. 'How much money is there in his bank account?'

But Anton had lost all interest in the conversation. He turned around without answering the question and walked to the SUV. They left the village without saying a word. He wanted to laugh, but the joke was on him. He had always looked down on the rustic villager as a drunken fool who couldn't even tell a man from a woman, falling in love with that ladyboy and losing his money on the casino floor.

But all this while, it was Balwant who had been laughing at him.

HUNGRY BIRDS FILLED THE BAY

Anton returned to Goa expecting serious repercussions. Instead, he found Bobby calmer than usual. He patiently heard him out without reprimanding him even once. But he did ensure that Anton recognised his culpability in the chain of events that had led to the fraud being committed. Once Anton had accepted his mistakes, he was let off mildly.

'Anton, we are human. We all make mistakes. But it is important that we learn from them and move on.'

This last statement put Anton at ease, and put to rest all his apprehensions. He went off to do his regular work with a light heart.

Bobby had spent the previous evening with Pankaj Adhikari narrating the whole sequence of events. Instead of telling Pankaj Adhikari that they had both been very cleverly played by Jayesh, Bobby had taken the easier way out and put the entire blame on Anton. He told Pankaj Adhikari that on several occasions in the past the online surveillance team had red flagged Balwant. But no further investigation was carried out because Anton had intervened and killed the enquiries. Similarly, when Bobby had doubts about enhanced credit limits being made available to Balwant, Anton had lobbied aggressively in favour of Balwant. Therefore, Anton was involved in the fraud. Pankaj Adhikari heard him out, but, he wasn't convinced.

'Bobby, all this evidence is circumstantial. It doesn't establish intent. Anton might be a brute, but he doesn't have the balls to do something like this. He knows only too well the price he would have to pay.'

'Boss, I knew you would to say that. I believed that too. But let me show you some hard evidence now. Evidence that cannot be refuted.' Bobby pulled out the photographs from the envelope. He had removed all photographs with Baldy in the picture. 'After the fraud involving the blackjack dealer, I had Anton tailed. He met the perpetrators of the fraud a few days later. I guess he was taking his cut.'

Pankaj Adhikari examined the photographs and didn't ask any further questions. Anton's fate was sealed.

Around 6:30 pm that evening, Anton got the first hint that all was not well. Bobby told him rather casually that Baldy had to go. Anton didn't know what he meant and argued that they couldn't let Baldy walk away.

'Not walk away,' replied Bobby. 'He needs to be fed to the fish. Make the arrangements.'

Anton was taken aback. But he did not know what he could say that would not bring suspicion on himself, so he decided to keep his reservations to himself. He wondered how he would deal with Jesse. Beating one of his guys was excusable, but feeding him to the fish was another matter altogether.

Anton went to the lockup where Baldy was still held in cuffs. The place stank of filth, as expected after holding a person for a fortnight. Baldy had recovered from much of the earlier beating. He lay in a corner of the lockup, in handcuffs.

The moment Anton entered, a tirade of filthy abuses was exchanged between them, involving almost the entire extended family. Baldy laughed aloud as Anton came closer to him and spat on his face. Anton immediately reciprocated by slapping him across his face.

'You don't scare me,' said Baldy. 'You will also die like a pig.'

Anton had no idea of the interaction between Bobby and Baldy. He was not smart enough to notice the confidence in Baldy's behaviour. Instead, he just lost his temper and slapped Baldy a few times across his face. Before Baldy could recover from the onslaught, he picked up a baseball bat that he had carried into the lockup and smashed Baldy's head from behind. It was all over within seconds.

Anton squatted on the floor beside the stationary body to see if he had finished the job. Chopping the body of a person who was still alive was beyond even his sensibilities. As he bent down to put his head on Baldy's chest, he heard a faint noise behind him. Startled, he raised his head to look around and saw the baseball bat being swung at him. He wanted to duck, but it was too late. Bobby wanted a clean hit and would have ideally hit him behind his head, but instead caught his face. The bat smashed into Anton's face with such fury that it crushed his jaw bone into small pieces and Anton collapsed on the ground.

Bobby knew that the job wasn't finished. He took another wild swing and smashed the back of Anton's head. This time he cracked his skull. He calmly put the bat on the ground. It was a long time since he had done something like this. He called two of his people, who had been specifically requisitioned from outside the casino, to take over. The bodies were dragged into the adjacent toilet and fed into a chopping machine that crushed meat and bones into mince. Bobby overlooked the entire operation and made sure that there was no trace left of Baldy or Anton.

After that the two bodies were mixed with bags of fresh fish bait and released into the bay under the darkness of the night. Half an hour later, the entire bay area came to life with thousands of excited sea gulls and other fish-eating birds circling the casino ship. They called and screeched as they dived in their hundreds to eat the fish that had swarmed the waters below.

Bobby came back to his room and poured himself a stiff drink. He swallowed it in a single go, then sat at his desk and began to think how the events of the last few days had unfolded. By putting the blame on Anton, he had not only absolved himself of any responsibility, but also provided Jayesh a clean chit, thereby unwillingly playing into his hands. He wasn't happy about that, but he had no choice. Pankaj Adhikari was unpredictable and could do anything. The wiser thing to do was to find a scapegoat to put the blame on.

Jayesh knew this. He knew that Bobby would never risk telling Pankaj Adhikari the truth and take part of the blame for what had happened. So, he had provided the photographs which acted as key evidence in closing the case and nailing Anton.

In the end, Bobby had survived and that was all that mattered. But the victory was bittersweet. He had to accept that he had been outplayed by a master player.

ALL FALL DOWN

They were still trying to figure out the quantity of money they had lost in the fraud, as one case after another emerged from each one of their casinos. The number was already more than $15 million.

They say that a cat has nine lives. Well, a politician has many more. He keeps resurrecting like a phoenix. Pankaj Adhikari was a seasoned politician. The fraud had hurt him, making him lose sleep for a few nights, but it hadn't derailed his resolve. Money could be earned again. But he had to ensure that something like this would never happen again. More than the lost money, he was worried about his reputation. He didn't want people to think that he had lost his edge. Some fool had decided to make good with money stolen from him. There had to be retribution. They would all have to pay.

It was time for him to reassert himself and remind them who was the boss. He went on a rampage against the other powerful families in the state to re-establish his position. Many people lost their lives, some for no fault of theirs. The drug mafia, including Jesse, went into hiding. Cops who didn't align themselves with Pankaj Adhikari were transferred overnight. Every underground activity in the state, from illegal mining to prostitution to drugs, came to a complete halt until a new order was established.

There was collateral damage with no clear victor. They all bled in this senseless war. But Pankaj Adhikari had convinced them that he had the wherewithal to outlast them. At last a broad truce was reached, the final contours of which were to be discussed on a weekend. Irrespective of their parties, they would once again drink whiskey from the same bottle.

It was at this time that Karishma came out with her well researched, front-page article about the nexus between Pankaj Adhikari and one of the largest casino chains in the country. The story was almost a biography, complete with photographs and snippets of personal letters. Had it not been negative, Pankaj Adhikari would have personally given accolades to Karishma for a job well done.

The story traced back Pankaj Adhikari's life from the time he was a small student union leader to the present. It delved into his relationship with Angela Da Rosa, his sweetheart of yesteryears, who later became popular as Jill. There were personal story accounts of how overzealous and possessive Pankaj Adhikari was about her. Then one day out of the blue, Angela Da Rosa became the defacto owner of the largest casino chain in the country. No one knew her background, or where her money had come from. The only thing of value was her relationship with Pankaj Adhikari. But soon the two of them fell apart as Pankaj Adhikari moved on to greener pastures to satiate his lust. So, she fell with the same swiftness that she had risen, losing her ownership of the casino business almost overnight to Jayesh Shah, who much like her, appeared out of the blue to acquire it. The story argued that all owners of the casino were fronts, or pawns, who were controlled and played by Pankaj Adhikari, who was the de facto beneficial owner of the casino chain.

The last paragraph of the story was nothing less than a tribute to Angela Da Rossa. It talked about her resolve to shed light on the murky operations of the casino business, knowing well that by doing so she was putting herself in danger. The last line said that Angela was missing for over a fortnight. The writer prayed for her wellbeing and hoped that she would show some proof of life upon reading this article.

For Pankaj Adhikari, the article couldn't have come at a worse time. He hadn't yet concluded his battle with his opponents. The only reason they had come to the negotiating table to agree on a truce was because they felt that he was in an advantageous position. This front-page article gave them ammunition to start a new battle on another front against Pankaj Adhikari and provided them with invaluable time to reorganise themselves. Within hours of the article being published, they backed off from the temporary truce and the weekend meeting was called off.

By afternoon almost every news daily, both print and television, had picked up the story. Reporters were everywhere, at the party headquarters, in front of Pankaj Adhikari's sprawling residence, and some even made it to the casino looking for that odd byte. Pankaj Adhikari was forced to remain within the confines of his house and plan his way out of this awkward situation. The first person he contacted was Bobby. 'Prepare for an enquiry by different government agencies,' he said. 'They should be coming any moment. They will be all over you like wild dogs. Don't worry. Stand your ground. I am working in the shadows.'

Bobby went to work immediately. He put the casino on a lockdown, suspended the launch service from the jetty, removed the receiving dock at the ship and put so much security in place that it would have taken a raiding party at least a few hours to board the ship. He then went on a spree, burning whatever documents he could lay his hands on. It was better not to have any documents at all than a wrong document falling into the hands of the government agencies.

After speaking with Bobby, Pankaj Adhikari went into damage control. He fixed up a meeting with the party treasurer in the afternoon. He knew that the best way forward was for him to be suspended, pending investigation. This would calm down public anger and deflect the heat from the party. People had very short memories, and it would all be forgotten in a few months. His donation to the party's coffers would ensure that nothing untoward was found in the investigations, paving the way for him to be re-inducted at a later date. They could even decide on the location of the welcoming ceremony.

It was only after his meeting with the party treasurer, that Pankaj Adhikari began calling his business opponents one by one. He told them that the party was behind him. He was willing to make concessions in good faith, but under no circumstances should his concessions be seen as a sign of weakness. By 4:00 pm that afternoon, Pankaj Adhikari had ensured status quo as it had existed on the prior evening.

He heaved a sigh of relief and sipped some tea as he made one final call. It was to his point man in the local police.

By evening, his political party had suspended him. The Department of Company Affairs had launched an investigation into the ownership of the casino. The local police had registered a missing person's report. It was all as Pankaj Adhikari had predicted.

Karishma arrived early at her office the next morning. She had spent all of the previous day waiting for her cell phone to ring, hoping that Jill would call. No call ever came and she had to finally accept the bitter truth. Jill had been done in by Pankaj Adhikari.

Her story was the biggest news in the country, but she found it difficult to be happy even though she was experiencing what was perhaps every journalists dream come true. She had failed to protect Jill. She had given her a false sense of security. She partly blamed herself for her disappearance and probable death. Was any story worth a life?

CHEERS TO BALI!

Ruby left for Phuket as soon as she was released from the hospital. She had always been confident, but now she felt a sense of completeness, a wholeness. It was as if a void had finally been filled. This is as far as present-day science and technology could have assisted her in her path towards womanhood. There was finally a compatibility between her mind and her body.

By evening, she was sitting beside Balwant on the Patong Beach sipping a cool Margarita. They were so comfortable together, holding hands, not a worry in the world. Whatever little anxiety she had about their relationship was gone. He had lived up to his part of the bargain. Not only that, he had done more for her than anyone else in her life.

But there were questions that he had to answer. Things had happened so fast that last night in Goa that she hadn't had any time to wait for every puzzle to be solved. She wasn't sure who he was. He was certainly no drunk. Even today, he held a glass of soda with a slice of lime. Then there was that bit about losing money. She had seen it with her own eyes and cried about it on many lonely nights. He said that he lost but didn't really lose. What the hell did that mean? Finally, how did he know exactly who she was?

She kept asking him questions but he refused to give her clear answers. He kept laughing at her. 'Have patience, darling,' he said. 'All your questions will be answered, but not by me.'

'Who will answer them?' she asked, a little irritated.

'You must have more faith, darling,' he said, grinning. 'Perhaps the angels will answer your queries.'

She kept asking him and he kept laughing at her and she slowly sipped one drink after another. Then a familiar whiff of sweet tobacco came floating on the air. She was still for a minute wondering if she was imagining it. But it came again and she turned around quickly. Jayesh Shah standing a few feet away from them. Ruby laughed delightedly, running to him in a slightly drunken haze, and to his surprise and embarrassment, hugged him. She apologised profusely for leaving Goa without telling him.

'No problem, Ruby,' said Jayesh, gently pushing her away. 'You did what you had to do.'

Then Jayesh turned to Balwant and hugged him. 'My dear friend,' he said. 'We finally meet without any pretence or stories.'

'She has many questions for you,' said Balwant, pointing at Ruby.

'I have all the time in the world to answer them,' replied Jayesh. 'Let's go to the dinner table, shall we?' he asked.

They sat around the dinner table late into the night. Ruby had so many questions. Jayesh answered them all.

'How do you two know each other?'

'We go back a long, long way. We started our gambling careers together.'

'But then you went on to run the casino?'

'Yeah! I told him that I didn't want to see him anywhere near my casino,' replied Jayesh. 'I put my sweat and blood in growing that casino.'

'One fine day, Jayesh called me out of the blue,' said Balwant. 'He sounded upset. I remember him telling me that he had tried to live an honest and fair life. But this world was not honest.'

'I felt cheated,' said Jayesh. 'I didn't understand why Adhikari wanted to pull the business away from me. I was the sole reason for its success.'

'So, we hatched a plan and put it into motion,' said Balwant.

'And that is when we met,' said Ruby.

'Yes,' replied Jayesh. 'I was confident that with you by Balwant's side, no one, especially Anton, would ever question his losing streak.'

'Now for one final question,' said Ruby. 'What is your real name, darling?'

'Balwinder,' replied Balwant.

'I will call you Bali,' she replied.

'Then Bali it is, my darling.'

'Cheers to Bali!'

AND THE WORLD GOES ON

Six months after the story about Pankaj Adhikari and his alleged links with the largest casino chain in the country had been published, Pankaj Adhikari won the elections comfortably as an independent candidate. Such was his hold on the politics in the state that the two main political parties had accommodated his candidature by fielding weak candidates against him. It was only because of the fear of public outcry that Pankaj Adhikari had not won the election unopposed.

The casino business was once again on the rise. After much noise, the investigations by the government agencies had gone cold. Some said that Bobby had paid off the officers in gold. Others speculated that Pankaj Adhikari had used his network to reach out to the higher-ups to have the investigations stalled. Whatever the reason, it was business as usual at the casino.

Jill was still missing. Since her body was never found, she continued to remain a missing person in the records of the police. Karishma was called to the police station almost every week to give attendance in the case.

Meanwhile, in Hong Kong, a group of three people who had recently arrived in the city were making waves on the racing track. Rumour had it that among them was a beautiful woman who was a whizz at identifying winners.

THE END